D1037674

# Bedfellow

# Bedfellow

## JEREMY C. SHIPP

A TOM DOHERTY ASSOCIATES BOOK

NEW YORK

This is a work of fiction. All of the characters, organizations, and events portrayed in this novella are either products of the author's imagination or are used fictitiously.

BEDFELLOW

Copyright © 2018 by Jeremy C. Shipp

Cover art by Greg Ruth

Hand-lettering by Greg Manchess

Cover design by Christine Foltzer

Edited by Lee Harris

A Tor.com Book
Published by Tom Doherty Associates
175 Fifth Avenue
New York, NY 10010

www.tor.com

Tor® is a registered trademark of
Macmillan Publishing Group, LLC.

ISBN 978-1-250-17528-1 (ebook)
ISBN 978-1-250-17529-8 (trade paperback)

First Edition: November 2018

*To my family*

# Bedfellow

# FRIDAY

## *Hendrick*

Hendrick prides himself on always responding well to an emergency, but he freezes in place when a man in a *Space Jam* nightshirt crawls through their living room window. The intruder carries a tattered grocery bag, which leaks a bright green ooze onto the hardwood floor. These floors are only two years old, Hendrick wants to tell the man, but of course he doesn't.

Instead, he says, "Go upstairs."

The man in the nightshirt tilts his head to the side, as if wondering why he should go upstairs at a time like this. But obviously Hendrick is speaking to his wife, who's sitting on the leather couch behind him. He can feel her fear emanating against his back, the same way he can sense her displeasure at a crowded office party.

"Imani, go," he says.

To be quite honest, Hendrick has often fantasized about a moment like this. On a date with his wife, Hendrick will imagine a man with a semiautomatic charging into the movie theater. In his mind, Hendrick will crawl through the aisle and lunge forward and burrow his thumbs into the terrorist's eyes.

In the here and now, Hendrick doesn't lunge forward. But he does take a step and point a threatening finger at the man's grimy face.

"Get the fuck out of my house," Hendrick says, proud of the line. He's feeling bolder by the second, because this *Space Jam* guy is obviously some poor, unarmed bastard who probably thinks he's in Narnia right now. Hendrick grew up in San Diego, and there he learned that homeless people are almost always harmless. He recalls a friend of his throwing an empty Dr Pepper can at an old man in a bright, pink robe, and the old man only whispered and turned away.

"Listen, buddy," Hendrick says, sounding a little too much like his father for his taste. "I don't want to call the police if I don't have to." In truth, he's already thinking about tonight's news report, where he's standing, slightly dazed in front of his house, the red and blue lights flashing on his face. Rosalita Little will come at him with her oversized microphone and say, "What inspired you to confront the intruder yourself, Mr. Lund?"

The nightshirt man responds to Hendrick's threat by smiling a little.

"Do you have *Howard the Duck* on Blu-ray?" the man

says, swinging his grocery bag gently from side to side. He speaks in a melodious, high-pitched voice that Hendrick finds offensive. "I heard there's a naked duck woman with boobs in that movie. Have you seen it?"

"I'm calling the police," Hendrick says, his Android already in his hand. "This is your last chance to get the fuck out of here."

"A DVD would be fine too, if you don't have a Blu-ray." The strange man sprays a line of green goo all over the floor with his damn swinging.

While Hendrick dials 911, the nightshirt man opens his grocery bag and stares inside with almost pupil-less eyes. What kind of drug does that to a person's eyes?

"Nine-one-one," the dispatcher says. "What's your emergency?"

Hendrick opens his mouth but his words catch in his throat like a craggy chunk of ice he accidentally swallowed. For one ridiculous moment, he considers asking the dispatcher why a duck would even have boobs when they're not mammals. This is a common enough occurrence for Hendrick, whose thoughts often veer left during somber situations like funerals or project meetings or arguments with his wife. He'll often burst into laughter and embarrass himself. He makes sure not to laugh now.

"Nine-one-one," the dispatcher says again.

"I think my bag is leaking," the homeless man says.

In an attempt at an even tone, Hendrick explains the situation and gives his address. He gives his address a second time, just in case.

Hendrick doesn't go upstairs and lock himself in a room with his family, as the dispatcher suggests. He strolls over to the fireplace and picks up the glass Coke bottle that someone (probably Kennedy) left on the mantelpiece. The girl never does pick up after herself.

The *Space Jam* guy studies Hendrick with his tiny eyes. "I've heard that Mexican Coke is better than the regular kind. Is that true?"

Hendrick stands at the bottom of the stairs, with his arms crossed over his chest. He waits. He can feel a rivulet of sweat trickling down his back, and part of him wishes for an end to all this. The other part isn't quite done yet.


## Kennedy


As a small child, Kennedy would navigate the world as an intrepid explorer, climbing cabinets and squeezing between fence posts and disappearing into clothing racks at the mall. Now, at thirteen years old, she still feels that whirling, staticky energy inside her. She sits on the bathroom tile, wriggling each of her toes, wanting to race downstairs to her dad.

"Has he texted you back yet?" Kennedy says.

"Not yet," her mom says, standing right next to the bathroom door. "I'm sure he's fine. The police will be here soon."

Her mother called the police hours (or was it minutes?) ago. Kennedy knows that some guy came into their house, but what disturbs her most is how quiet and still her house has become. She expected yelling, screaming, struggling. Instead, she can't hear anything from downstairs. Her mom and brother are hardly moving. Even the wind outside seems to have died down since they locked themselves in here. The girl realizes her thoughts are running rampant in her head, and she's being ridiculous, but the silence of her home still disquiets her.

Sitting beside her, Tomas hands her an ant in a top hat drawn on his yellow notepad. Drawing Battle often begins with an insect or a mouse. Kennedy takes the ballpoint pen and starts sketching an anthropomorphic shoe that could smash the ant. Next, Tomas will draw a ball of flame or any object or creature that could destroy the shoe, and the game will go on from there. Kennedy doesn't consider herself much of an artist, and her turns tend to last a minute or less. Tomas, on the other hand, will strain himself to create a moon with craters for eyes and mountain ranges for lips. He'll spawn a giant robotic jerboa crushing New York City. He'll always end the game by drawing God, who, depending on the day, will turn out to be a Gandalf-looking wizard or a hippo vomiting a swirling galaxy.

After Kennedy finishes her cross-eyed shoe, she stands and cracks her knuckles.

"Can you not?" her mother says, still tapping at her phone.

Kennedy is bewildered by the fact that her mother could worry about knuckle-cracking at a time like this, but her mother often surprises her in this way.

"Has he texted yet?" the teenager says.

"No," her mother says, with a small quiver in her voice. "I'll let you know when he does."

At the sound of the small quiver, the static inside Kennedy whirls faster. She imagines her father lying on the hardwood floor downstairs, being silently strangled by a man in a black ski mask. Kennedy sidesteps her brother and slowly reaches out to touch the brass handle of the bathroom door.

Before her mother notices what's happening, Kennedy scrambles outside and surges down the hallway. Eventually, she slows and turns her head.

From here, Kennedy can see her father sitting motionless at the bottom of the stairs. The man who broke in isn't wearing a ski mask after all. He's sitting cross-legged on the floor, wearing a Bugs Bunny shirt.

The man glances up at Kennedy and gives a little wave.

Her dad stands and turns around.

"Go to your mom," he says, and he sounds calm. He looks a bit sweaty but Kennedy can't see any cuts or bruises.

When someone grabs her arm, Kennedy half expects another man in a matching Bugs Bunny shirt to be standing beside her. But it's only her mother.

Her mother mouths a couple words that Kennedy doesn't catch and pulls her back down the hall. Twisting away, the teenager slips into Tomas's bedroom. She heads straight for the closet, where she finds her brother's stubby aluminum bat.

This time, when her mother leads her back to the bathroom, she follows.

"What were you thinking?" her mother whispers, still holding her arm with a hand like a metal claw.

Kennedy wriggles herself free. "Dad's okay, I think. The guy who broke in was just sitting there."

Her mother continues to stand beside her, obviously on guard in case her daughter tries to make a run for it again. Kennedy glances at her brother and notices that he's staring at the bat in her hand.

"Just in case," she says.

Her brother shifts his gaze to his notepad. He dangles his pen over the paper without drawing anything.

"Did the man have a gun?" her mother says, quietly.

"I didn't see one," the teenager says.

The three of them sit in silence for a while, and the cypress stands motionless outside the high bathroom window.

Kennedy thinks about the unwashed man on the floor, and about her father's tirades whenever he spots someone giving money to a homeless person. He'll only get worse after tonight. He'll say, "Great, give that guy some drug money so he can tweak out and break into our house like the last guy." Kennedy almost wishes the man on the floor were a well-groomed thief with a mustache, like in an old British film.

"Give me the bat, honey," her mother says.

Kennedy studies her mother for a moment, and then hands over the squat little weapon. Her mother rests the bat across her lap. She taps at her violet, furry phone.

Tomas hands over his notepad, and Kennedy wonders who could defeat this shoe-eating ninja goat? A tyrannosaurus samurai? The teenager scribbles on the next blank piece of paper. When she stretches out her legs and wiggles her toes, the wind picks up again. The cypress sways in the tiny window above. She thought the movement would make her feel less uneasy, would make the whirling static lull a little in her limbs, but she was wrong.

## Imani

With a sense of dread, Imani scrolls backward in time through the digital albums on her phone. Her crow's feet vanish, and her children shrink smaller and smaller until they disappear altogether. Her husband's gray hairs become imbued with the color of the sequoia trees she would jokingly hug during their camping trips. "I'm a tree hugger," she would say, every time. As she rewinds their lives together, Hendrick also appears increasingly happy. More often, he grins with his whole face and he gives his stupid double thumbs-up to the camera. Imani slows down at a picture of the two of them standing in front of a dark green pond, a duckling balanced on Hendrick's palm. She told him not to pick up the duck, but he did anyway.

But none of this is the point of Imani's search. When the man in the nightshirt first appeared, standing behind the open bay window, he winked at her, knowingly. And she recognized him.

Imani scrolls through the albums with a trembling thumb, but she can't find the man anywhere. She's afraid that he knew her during her wilder days, back when she didn't take many pictures. Did she wrong him somehow? For so many years, Imani has pretended to be a nice, normal mother and a nice, normal wife. Of course a man would crawl out of the past to punish her for this charade.

Imani attempts to jostle these thoughts out of her with a shake of her head. She's being silly. The man downstairs is no one, and she didn't even get a good look at his face, anyway. How could she recognize him at all?

She continues to search through her photos until Hendrick finally texts back with, Everything's fine.

For a second, she strokes the furry phone with googly eyes, as if in thanks for the good news.

"Your dad says everything's okay," Imani says, standing from the closed toilet. "I'm going to check and see what's happening. You two stay here and lock the door behind me."

"Can't I come with you?" her daughter says, already standing.

"I cannot toilet you do that," the mother says, because she wants her home to feel normal and stupid again.

The girl presses her hands against the sides of her face. "That was horrible."

Imani shrugs. "Stay here."

She leaves, almost tripping as she steps over her son's legs, and she takes the baseball bat with her. Thankfully, she hears the soft click of the lock behind her.

On her more stressful days, Imani will sometimes drive over a bump in the road with her Flux, and she'll have to look back to make sure she didn't hit a raccoon or a cat or a human being who happened to be lying flat on the street in the dark. And if she doesn't look back, she'll picture a half-dead possum dangling under her car, his flesh scraping against the road, until she can get home and check. Tonight, while she makes her way through the hall, she pictures a man leaping out from one of the bedrooms. And after she swings wildly with the bat, she realizes too late that she's smashed Hendrick in the face, his nose gnarled, his teeth tumbling down a waterfall of blood. She attempts to quiet her imagination with a few deep breaths.

From the stairs, she can hear guttural whispers coming from the living room, but when she makes her way down, she realizes what she's hearing is the crackling of a fireplace on the TV. Her husband loves the sound of fire, and he'll often play one of these damn videos while reading or playing one of his silly phone games.

"Hendrick?" she says, pausing at the bottom of the stairs.

"Everything's fine," he says, echoing his text.

She finds her husband with his bare feet on their oversized ottoman, as if a man didn't invade their home only minutes ago. He's caressing an Old Fashioned ornamented with a maraschino cherry and an orange wheel. He only adds the fruit during special occasions. Imani despises Old Fashioneds with a passion, so she assumes the second cocktail on the serving tray isn't meant for her.

"What happened?" Imani says.

Her husband taps at the side of his glass with an index finger and gives a sheepish-looking smile. "It was all a stupid misunderstanding." He turns down the sound of the fire slightly with the remote. "Marvin tried ringing the doorbell, but it's not working, apparently. So, then he tried knocking, but we couldn't hear him over the TV. That's why he came over to tap on the window."

Imani does like to up the volume of the TV to nearly earth-shattering levels. She remembers the man at the window tapping on the glass, and she remembers screaming. She remembers saying, *"What the fuck is that? What the fuck is that?"*

Hendrick shakes his head and sighs. "You screamed and I went into full papa bear mode. I still can't believe I called the police. Fuck. They came to the door, and I had to explain everything. Marvin's still shaken up."

At this point, Imani glances around the room for this so-called Marvin, half expecting him to be crouching in a corner, watching all of this unfold. The name *Marvin* sounds very familiar somehow, and the wife is even more convinced that he's some weirdo from her past.

"He was trying to come inside," Imani says, the artificial fire still sputtering at her back.

Hendrick shakes his head and then takes another sip of his drink. A bit of the liquid spills onto his T-shirt. "He tapped on the window and you screamed because we were watching that fucking serial killer show. You know how you get."

Imani remembers Marvin standing at the window, tapping at the glass. She thought he winked at her, but it could have been a blink. He could have been tapping and blinking and nothing more.

When Marvin strolls out of the downstairs bathroom, Imani feels a sudden urge to bash his head in with the bat or run outside, or one and then the other. The feeling almost instantly collapses, however. His clean-cut look comes as a relief to her, with his excessively gelled side-part and his collared button-up patterned with blurry white stars. She doesn't know exactly what she was expecting to see when he stepped out of the bathroom, but this is not it.

"Hey there," he says, and he takes a seat next to Hendrick. He puts his feet up on the ottoman, right next to her husband's. "You have a beautiful home. The layout kind of reminds me of the house from *Troll*. Have you seen it?"

"No," Imani says.

"It's no *Troll 2* but it's pretty good." Marvin takes a sip of his cocktail, and judging by his expression, he enjoys Old Fashioneds as much as Imani does. "You know what's weird? In *Troll,* the main character is a little boy named Harry Potter who ends up doing magic. No one ever believes me when I say that, but it's true."

By now, Imani's feeling like a complete idiot, because she's finally remembered where she knows this guy. He's the man who gave Tomas the Heimlich earlier that day. When Tomas started choking, Marvin seemed to appear out of nowhere, softly lit in the dim steakhouse. He wore the same dark dress pants and starfield shirt. Imani was so focused on Tomas that she hardly looked at the man who saved him. She thanked him, again and again, but she kept her eyes on her son.

Marvin is here, of course, because Hendrick must have invited him over for a drink. Hendrick will often invite work friends over without telling Imani, which annoys the hell out of her when she's not in the mood to entertain.

"Thank you for what you did," Imani says. "You really saved the day."

"I guess I'm a regular Mighty Mouse," Marvin says, pushing the cocktail away from himself a little with a single finger.

A commercial for constipation medicine interrupts the YouTube video of the fireplace. Imani doesn't turn around to look, but she can only assume that a talking piece of shit is the one shouting, "I'm melting. What a world. What a world."

Imani feels compelled to pour herself a drink of her own, but she doesn't.

"Oh," she says. "I should get the children. They're still in the bathroom." Immediately, she feels like a monster for leaving them there for so long.

On her way up the stairs, the crackling of the fireplace once again sounds like a murmuring of sharp, urgent consonants. "Ks ksh tss," the voices say. In the hall, she realizes that she's still gripping the small aluminum bat. Right as she's about to toss the toy onto her son's bedroom floor, she changes her mind. Instead, she places the weapon under her bed, on her side, next to her little porcelain box of worthless treasures. Imani laughs at herself for being such a panicky fool, but she's still frightened. She's not frightened of Marvin, of course. She's afraid of the man in her imagination who still might be out there, squatting in the dark, waiting to push open the living room window so that he can crawl inside.

## Tomas

Luckily for Tomas, he managed to grab a handful of pens before his mother dragged him into the bathroom and said, in a terrified voice, that everything would be fine. Now, while waiting for his sister to finish her drawing, he organizes his pens into a rainbow of sorts. Auburn, tangerine, chartreuse, citron, emerald, ube, lilac, imperial purple.

Tomas understands that there are men in the world who wear masks and rob houses, but what Tomas doesn't understand is why one of these men would break into a home like theirs. Why steal from children when you can go after guys like Prince John or Voldemort? The boy can only assume that the thief broke into their house by mistake, never suspecting that he was interrupting a family's Fun Friday.

"Okay, done," his sister says, and hands him the notepad.

Tomas studies the drawing for a few moments. "What is this guy?"

"Tyrannosaurus samurai."

"His head looks like a duck head."

"Well, he's a tyrannosaurus. See, he's got short little arms. He can't swing the sword very well, but he manages to squish your goat."

Tomas nods approvingly. While the dinosaur makes quick work of the ninja duck and the surrounding farm animals, the boy ponders his next move. He could of course send out an F-16 Fighting Falcon, but to be honest, he's tired of drawing machines. These days, he's more interested in natural-looking killing machines, like crab dragons or moss men who vomit poisonous mushrooms.

Back on the farm, the T. rex awkwardly sheaths his katana and then bursts through a white picket fence into the open countryside. The boy decides to send forth a half-barn half-vampire hybrid to deal with the creature, but there's a knock at the door before he can even grab a pen.

"It's me," his mom says, her voice muffled through the door. "Everyone's safe. Everything's fine."

Kennedy's already out the door by the time Tomas finishes collecting his makeshift rainbow.

"The man from the restaurant is here," his mom says. "You should come down and thank him."

Of course, when his mom says that he should do something, what she means is that he will. She stands by the door, watching him with eyes of burnt umber.

Downstairs, Tomas slips on a wet spot on the floor, but he manages to keep himself upright.

"Be careful, sweetie," his mom says.

"Ah, here's the man of the hour," his father says, raising his glass. Tomas isn't sure what he means by this, but the boy smiles a little nonetheless.

His mom says, "Tomas wanted to thank you for what you did."

The stranger crouches in the corner, studying their bookshelf of Blu-rays. Tomas doesn't understand why the man is wearing his dad's pelican shirt, but a moment later, he realizes that the tiny pelicans on the shirt are actually white blobs.

"Thank you," Tomas says.

"No prob." The stranger turns around, holding a copy of *Return to Oz*. "Hey, have you seen this one?"

"Only a little," the boy says. The truth is that while he can easily face his own creations, Tomas can't handle every creature he comes across. He cried when he saw the Wheelers, and his mom said he didn't have to watch the rest of the movie.

"How is it compared to *Wizard of Oz*?" the stranger says.

"It's scarier," the boy says.

"Hmm." The man returns the Blu-ray to the shelf and continues his search.

Tomas stands silent, staring at the back of the man's shirt, unsure as to whether he's expected to say more. He glances at his mom, but she's busy whispering in his dad's ear. His dad looks half-asleep on the couch, with his glass tucked between his legs.

While staring at the stranger, Tomas notices a smudge in his vision. He attempts to wipe at his glasses with his T-shirt, but this doesn't help. Maybe he needs to run his glasses under the faucet.

"I made you yours," Kennedy says, appearing beside him with a hot fudge sundae in each hand.

The boy studies his bowl, to make sure the ice cream to whipped cream ratio is correct. Yes, his whipped cream reigns supreme.

"Thanks," he says.

His sister disappears up the stairs, as if washed away by some invisible river. Sometimes, Tomas wishes he could be more like his sister and leave any room with such ease.

"Is there any more of that?" the stranger says, motioning at the sundae with a DVD copy of *Big Trouble in Little China*. The case slips out of his hand and he says, "Agh."

Tomas stares into his bowl, as if searching for the answer. "I don't know," he says. "You could look in the freezer."

"That's not mint chocolate chip, is it?"

"No."

While the man retrieves the dropped DVD, Tomas sidesteps in the direction of the stairs. His mother doesn't tell him to stop. His father's eyes are closed, his fingers interlaced over his belly. The man doesn't ask any more questions about the ice cream, so Tomas manages to escape upstairs without any problems. A muffled version of David Bowie's gnome song leaks out of his sister's closed door. For a moment, Tomas considers joining his sister. She would let him sit on her bed and eat his ice cream. She would show him YouTube videos of a dancing baby or a dog and an elephant who are best friends.

In the end, Tomas decides on the peace and quiet of his own tidy sanctuary. On Fun Friday, not only can he eat a whipped cream sundae in his Mechagodzilla pajamas, but he can stay up until ten p.m. Unfortunately, a cloud of fatigue is already diffusing throughout his arms and legs. It's only a matter of minutes before the fog will spread up into his eyes.

With little time to spare, Tomas wriggles half of his body under his bed so that he can reach his drawing journal. Mrs. Z gave him the journal last year, on the last day of school. She told him the rules of the journal. She also said that if he ever filled up the journal, he could come back to her classroom, and she would give him another. He remembers the tiny cerulean smiley faces painted on her fingernails that day.

Tomas's first instinct is to capture a quiet moment in the bathroom, his mom staring at a black blot of spider on the wall, his sister gnawing at the top button of her flannel shirt. At the time, Tomas didn't feel particularly frightened of the robber in the house. He trusted that his father could throw the man out the front door, if necessary. He didn't understand why his mom and sister seemed so nervous.

The boy's pen lowers slightly but hovers a millimeter above the paper. He finds himself suddenly overwhelmed by a sense of obligation to the man in the restaurant. The man did save his life, didn't he? Doesn't he deserve at least one page of Tomas's memories?

The boy gazes into the bright, white paper, and he sends his consciousness back through time, into Thomas's Bar & Grill. He has no particular fondness for the Fun Guy Burger and Crazy Fries he always orders; he likes that his mother never fails to say, "Let's go to your restaurant, Tomas." He likes the fake, flickering candles on the table, and he likes the artificial oak tree in the center of the restaurant, decorated with fairy lights and a hodgepodge of dangling ornaments. Tomas can remember when Kennedy would walk with him around the tree before the food arrived, and they would find their favorite ornaments: the banjo-playing flamingo and the glittery pinecone and the ugly pineapple man. Now Kennedy won't walk around the tree anymore.

Tomas remembers the moments before the chunk of hamburger clung inside his throat, too afraid to drop down into his stomach. He doesn't blame the hamburger, really. He wouldn't want to be digested in a pool of acid either. Before Tomas started choking, his sister carefully balanced another butter packet on her tower of condiments. His dad accidentally said "fucking Brendan" instead of "freaking Brendan," and his mom's eyes widened into little UFOs. "Hendrick Lund," she said.

When Tomas began choking, he sat very still with his palms flat on the paper tablecloth. He studied his father's rosy, smirking face.

"Tomas?" his mom said. "Something's wrong with him. Tomas, say something."

By the time his father stood up, Tomas already felt his body rising up and up off his chair. An arm wrapped around his stomach and squeezed, like the tentacle of an angry octopus. As he hovered in the air, the restaurant swirled around him and the fairy lights on the oak tree blurred into shooting stars. The hamburger piece flew out of him, landing next to his sister's unused knife.

His mother held him then, and when he looked at her, the edges of her face quivered. "Thank you," she said. "Thank you." Tomas faced the stranger, and the line of the man's mouth became jagged like the seismograph he saw on his last field trip. The stars on the man's shirt twinkled as if they were real.

Back in his room again, Tomas feels his heart slamming against his chest, again and again. A hot tear burns his right eye. *I should . . .* he thinks, but the thought crumbles into nothingness.

Before he can formulate a plan of action, the boy finds himself in the hallway, heading for his parents' room. He can still see his mother's face in the restaurant, her skin rippling, her eyes twisted like silly putty. Inside, he screams, *Go away! Go away!*

Before the boy can reach his parents' bedroom, he notices that the guest room door is wide open, and he hears someone on the TV say, "No one laughs at a master of Quack Fu." Tomas doesn't understand why anyone would be watching TV in there. His grandparents only visit during Christmas.

Tomas strolls forward and glances as casually as possible into the guest room. Through smudged glasses and a weepy right eye, Tomas sees a man standing alone by the TV. This isn't his grandfather. Without leaning over, the man stretches a pale arm to pick a bottle off the floor. The man turns and stares at Tomas with pupils that are little more than amaranth-colored pinpricks. When the man opens his mouth, Tomas screams.

"Oh, hey, kid," the man says. "Scream scream to you, too."

After wiping the tears from his eyes, Tomas sees the man from the restaurant standing by the TV, holding a plastic grocery bag. He pulls a Gatorade out of the bag and adds the drink to a line of bottles on the windowsill. Now his hazel eyes appear perfectly boring.

"I'm going to see my mom," the boy says, because he's not sure what else he can say.

"Cool," the man says, pulling another Gatorade from his tattered bag. A miniscule waterfall of bright green liquid spills onto the floor from the bottom of the bottle. Tomas feels a mild urge to tell the man that the hardwood is only two years old, like his dad always says, but he keeps his mouth shut.

"Ah, here's the culprit," the man continues. He lifts the bottle to his lips and drinks from the lesion in the plastic, as if he's sucking poison from a rattlesnake bite. His Adam's apple dances up and down.

While the man is busy, Tomas takes this opportunity to sidestep in the direction of his parents' room. For some reason, unknown even to Tomas himself, he's always held a deep-seated belief that holding your breath can spawn an invisible bubble around your body. You aren't invulnerable within the bubble, of course. But you are luckier. You can sometimes walk through the hallways at school without so much as a flick to your shoulder. With all this in mind, Tomas holds his breath now.

"Hey," the man says, rupturing the bubble with a small, jagged word. "Has anyone ever told you that you look like that kid from *Flight of the Navigator*? Not so much your hair, but the shape of your face. Your nose, I guess. Did you know that kid ended up robbing a bank? Not in the movie, I mean. Real life. Would it be weird if I called you David, like the character?"

"That's not my name," Tomas says.

"Okay, well." The man tosses the empty Gatorade bottle onto the floor. "You seem a little on edge, what with that screaming fit of yours earlier. I mean, I get it. There's a new guy staying in your house and you don't know him from Adam, whoever the fuck Adam is. Agh, sorry for cursing." He taps an index finger against his forehead. "So, uh, your mom told me you like to draw. I knew a woman once who painted cats as clowns. It really helped her relax. Maybe you could draw for a while and try to chill out a little bit."

Finally, Tomas manages to break free from the restaurant man's gaze and stumble away from his line of sight. More than anything, he wants to tell his parents about his mother's gnarled eyes in the restaurant. He wants to tell them about the man's body. But his father will only tell him to calm down. He'll say, "This house is a no-drama zone." He'll say, "Come back when you're ready to tell the truth."

Instead of knocking, Tomas runs his hands over the squares of molding on his parents' ivory door. Their murky voices sound a world away. Tomas heads back the way he came, and this time he keeps his eyes focused forward. When he passes the guest room, he imagines the man's long, snaking arms reaching for his neck. Tomas holds his breath.

## Hendrick

His wife doesn't so much pace the room as ping-pong from wall to wall, straightening a perfectly straight lampshade, reorganizing the army of LED candles on her bedside table.

"The man's house is being fumigated," Hendrick says, lying flat on their velvet quilt. He knows he should take off his oxfords, but that would likely cause him to fall asleep instantly. "Instead of watching him drive off drunk to get a motel room in the middle of the night, I thought this would be the polite thing."

In truth, Hendrick's more than a little buzzed himself, and he can't quite recall the precise moment he invited Marvin to stay the night. Nevertheless, the offer was made, and he's not about to backstep now.

"He could have called an Uber," Imani says, searching through her sock-and-underwear drawer.

"You're right, but the guy saved our son's life. I thought we could do him a favor." Hendrick sits up and turns himself so that his feet hover over the edge of the bed. "Honestly, though, this isn't about the guy. This is about you freaking out again. You project your mom onto every new person you meet, so you never want to give them a chance. At least admit to yourself that that's true."

"Thanks, babe," Imani says, to a section of empty wall. "I love it when you throw my childhood in my face like that. Real classy."

"I'm not throwing anything." He lies on his back a little too fast, and the ceiling swirls above him. "The point . . . the point is that you're not the best judge of character. You think everyone's a secret cannibal. You don't even want the kids to go to sleepovers."

The sound of shattering glass pervades Hendrick's consciousness.

"Fuck," Imani says. "That was an accident. I'm not throwing things. I broke my little porcelain peanut guy."

"I'm sorry."

He sits up and watches her pick up pieces of the smiling peanut using two fingers.

"I'm all for judging Marvin fairly," she says. "But we don't know him. I get inviting him over for a drink, but you should talk with me first before you ask a stranger to stay the night."

"But he's not exactly a stranger, is he? We talked with him for who knows how long at the restaurant. He told us his whole damn life story. You said you liked the guy."

Imani stays frozen for a moment and then rubs her face with both hands. She leaves a trail of blood from her forehead to her chin.

"You're bleeding," Hendrick says.

His wife studies her hands. "Fuck."

When she returns from the bathroom with a poop-emoji Band-Aid on her finger, she says, "Marvin does seem like a good person, and yeah, we had a nice long conversation about his hippie parents and his Chihuahuas. Even so, we don't really know him." She sighs. "But I suppose it's too late to kick him out now. I'm going to check on the kids."

Hendrick lies back with his oxfords on, because he still wants to visit the basement tonight. He enjoys creeping through the darkness while the rest of his world sleeps, and pulling the false bricks from the basement wall. Despite all his best efforts, Hendrick falls asleep on the gunmetal velvet. In the dream that follows, the basement fills with murky water and a pale serpent wraps around his face, painlessly. He asks Imani to take a picture but she won't turn around. She says he can take his own damn picture. She says he's as good as dead.

## *Kennedy*

Traditionally, Kennedy spends her Fun Fridays watching videos where a family of squirrel monkeys rides on a capybara, or a Canadian woman bakes a tiny chocolate cake for her hamster's birthday, or anything in that vein. However, her plans change when she's drenched in a wave of realization that she hates her room. She absolutely despises this place, and the truth of the matter is that she's felt this way for a very long time.

For about half an hour, Kennedy sits at her hand-painted rainbow desk, drawing plans for a room-wide re-design. In one plan, her collection of stuffed penguins dangles from the ceiling on strings. Twinkle lights coil up the legs of her scrapbooking table. And posters of Hogwarts and Wonder Woman and David Bowie form a madcap collage on the opposite wall. As soon as she finishes a plan, she crumples the paper and tosses it into the open mouth of her Totoro wastepaper basket. Each permutation is worse than the last.

The problem, she decides, is that she's living not so much in a bedroom but a mausoleum of abandoned hobbies and forgotten dreams. Maybe she's being a little overdramatic, but the truth is that she doesn't give a crap about her scrapbooking table or her saxophone or even most of her posters. She doesn't want to throw any of this stuff away, because the thought makes her want to cry.

Ultimately, she puts away her astronaut cat notebook and opens her laptop. The first perfect video that she comes across is of a Sphynx who won't stop meowing until her human places a glittery, violet cowboy hat on her head. She swiftly opens up the same video on her phone and heads for Tomas's room. In truth, she's going not only to show him the Sphynx (as well as the enormous possum who bites an old man's arm) but to check on him. While she's not particularly frightened of Marvin, she still feels a faint swirling energy in her limbs that makes her want to run laps around the house or punch a wall. On a conscious level, she knows her family isn't in any danger. Nevertheless, she can't stop thinking about the imaginary man in the black ski mask. In the back of her mind, he's in her brother's room right now, pointing a butcher knife at his eye.

Thankfully, she finds her brother alone, playing on his computer, wearing his massive orange headphones. He looks even smaller than usual in those headphones, sitting on their dad's hand-me-down office chair.

"Tomas," she says. "Tomas!"

The boy jumps in his seat and spins around. With a glance at her phone, he pauses his flying goat game and rolls his chair to the side of the bed, without ever standing up. Kennedy sits cross-legged on the Steven Universe blanket. She shows him the possum video first, since it's the less important of the two.

While her brother watches, Kennedy gazes past him at the spiral of yellow sticky notes that blazon the wall with miniature coats of arms. There's a jerboa in chainmail with a blue-and-white background. There's an upside-down house with a bigfoot gripping the chimney for dear life. Kennedy once asked if these little escutcheons mean anything, and he said no. Ordinarily, she experiences nothing but a mild sense of pride when looking at her brother's artwork. Tonight, she suffers a few pangs of jealousy. He knows what he likes, and he has the capacity to stay interested in an activity for more than a few weeks at a time. Worst of all, he makes it look so easy.

Thankfully, the envy dissipates as soon as she focuses on her phone once again.

"Is that possum his pet?" Tomas says. "Can you have possums as a pet?"

"I dunno," Kennedy says. "I have another good one."

Partway through the cat video, their mom interrupts for the millionth time tonight. She's wearing her dancing-taco nightgown.

"Everything fine and dandy in here?" their mother says.

"Great," Kennedy says, tossing her flip-flop a few feet using two of her toes. "I smoked a pack of cigarettes, and all of Tomas's teeth fell out."

"All his teeth, huh?" their mom says. She leans back against the doorframe, her arms crossed over her chest. "That sounds flossome."

"Mom, no."

"It hurts me when you lie like that. I've got fillings too, you know?"

After Kennedy tosses her second flip-flop across the room, she looks up, and her mom's already disappeared. As Kennedy shows her brother the rest of the cat video, he casually pinches a few of his teeth. The video ends, and he rubs his right eye, smiling.

"That cat should ride on a little horse," he says, yawning in the middle of the sentence. "She could use her yarn for like a . . . a cowboy rope. A lasso."

"That would be cool," Kennedy says. She takes a circuitous route to the door, collecting her flip-flops and wearing them on her hands. For a moment, she considers walking on all fours like a horse but ultimately decides against it.

As soon as she passes through the doorway, she hears, "Did you find any other videos?"

Kennedy freezes and then walks backward into the room, as if someone's pressed Rewind on reality. She even tosses her shoes on the floor, where they were, to enhance the effect. Tomas isn't paying any attention to her, though. He's spinning around slowly in his office chair with his eyes half-closed.

"Do you want to go to bed?" the girl says. "You're already asleep. You're sleep-spinning."

"I'm not."

Kennedy hops onto the bed and take out her phone. She taps the screen on and off and on again. "No one's gonna break into the house, you know? It was just a misunderstanding, like Dad said. Marvin tapped on the window and Mom freaked out. That was it."

After a few seconds, Tomas slows to a stop, facing a shelf of ceramic skulls and dragons. "Mom's face looked weird in the restaurant," he says. "Her eyes looked mushed."

Kennedy feels her heart climbing up into her throat. "What do you mean?"

"Her skin kept moving," he whispers. "The man looked weird too."

"What are you talking about?"

"In the restaurant, when the hamburger got stuck. Everything was wavy and mushed."

Kennedy taps her phone gently against her knee. "Well, I mean, when you choked, your brain probably freaked out or something. Mom's eyes were never mushed. I was there too. Everything was normal, except for the burger chunk that flew out of your mouth a hundred miles an hour."

He's facing her now, his eyes more awake than a minute ago. "Can I stay in your room tonight?"

"All right," Kennedy says. "But no egg farts, okay? The last time you egg farted, I almost died."

The boy grabs his Stay Puft Marshmallow Man head pillow and follows her into her room. For a while, they listen to Bowie's "Magic Dance" on repeat, and tragically, Tomas does end up releasing one of his more severe egg farts. Kennedy pretends to die in her bed. Her last words are "Avenge . . . me."

Tomas falls asleep first, curled up on a cloud of ultra-plush blankets on her floor. His sister makes sure that his chest is still moving before turning away.

Sitting on her bed, she takes one last grim look at her room and decides that what she needs is the holodeck from her dad's *Star Trek* show. She needs a room that's decorated with illuminated manuscripts and K-pop album covers one day and Wonder Woman memorabilia the next. She needs a room that can keep up. Kennedy closes her eyes and tries not to think about her mother with mushed eyes and moving skin. She commands her brain not to dream of it. Soon, she's outside and Tomas is up high in an oak tree, a pale branch impaled through his chest. She tells him not to keep climbing, because that will only make the hole inside him bigger, but he won't listen. He won't stop climbing until he reaches the top.

# SATURDAY

## *Imani*

When Imani discovers that her son's room is empty at four thirty in the morning, she pictures him bound with bright red cable ties, trapped in an oil-stained trunk. The image wraps around her consciousness until she checks her daughter's room and finds Tomas sprawled like a doll on the floor. His hand's resting on one of his sister's orange Havaianas. Meanwhile, Kennedy's sleeping serenely in an erratic tangle of limbs and blankets and body pillows. To make an attempt at unscrambling her at this point would only wake her up. Imani leaves them be, and gazes at them for a while from the doorframe. She hopes they're dreaming of candy houses and puppies, and not the featureless face that haunted her through the night.

Once she turns away from her children, she notices that the guest room door now stands wide open. It was closed only a minute ago. Before she can decide whether or not she should take a glance inside, she hears the distinctive and disheartening sound of a man violently vomiting. Imani herself feels the jagged claws of a headache squeezing the back of her skull with every step she takes. She often wakes up with headaches, particularly when she doesn't get enough sleep, but she's still worried that she's the next in line to violently vomit out her insides.

Despite all of her anxieties, Imani looks in on Marvin and finds him sitting on the edge of the bed, olive-green vomit splattered on the Persian-inspired rug she ordered from eBay.

"Hey," Marvin says. "Sorry for Linda Blairing all over everything."

After one of her children vomits, Imani likes to say, "What's up, Chuck? How are you feeling?" This time, however, she decides to travel a different path.

"Don't worry about it," Imani says. The way Marvin's sitting there, slumped forward with his hands on his knees, reminds her of her brother during those last few months in the hospital. The thick, dark rings under his eyes look more like bruises, as if someone punched each side of his face.

"I should get going," Marvin says. "But I was wondering if I could try sleeping some of this off? Just a few hours maybe would get me on my feet again."

"Do you want me to drive you to urgent care?"

He waves away the thought with a slight raising of his

hand. "Nah, I think this is just the flu my mom had recently. Nothing too deadly."

"You get some sleep," Imani says, crossing her arms over her chest. "Can I get you anything? Water? Tylenol? Holy water?"

"Nah, I'm fine." He says this lying on his back, with his eyes closed. By the time Imani returns with her pink surgical mask and a box of baking soda, Marvin's snoring like her sleep apnea–suffering grandfather. Quietly, Imani uses towel after towel to remove as much vomit as possible off the rug.

"Howard, stop," Marvin grumbles, between snores.

As she blots away the pea soup–green moisture, her headache travels from the back of her head to the front, pulsing in steady bursts of bright red pain. She pictures a jaundiced tumor, twisted and wrinkled, in the shape of a featureless face. She shakes her head, admonishing her own mind. After the rug is moderately dry, she sprinkles the baking soda on top. That should do the trick.

Before exiting, Imani takes one last look at Marvin, to confirm that he's not vomiting in his sleep or bleeding from the eyes or something worse. The poor man's no longer snoring. Each protracted exhale brings with it an audible sigh. "Haaaaaaaaaa," he says, as if he's performing some new-age meditation.

Imani closes the door silently, to contain the illness as

much as possible. Next, she descends into the basement in order to deposit the vomit rags into the washing machine. One of the plastic storage boxes has been moved off the stack into the middle of the basement. One of the kids must have been playing down here. Without thinking, Imani begins collecting the clothes from the rest of the house. Technically, it's Hendrick's turn to do the laundry, but once again, he's allowed all the hampers to overflow. As she works, she seethes, and she feels petty for allowing herself to get so worked up. She knows, of course, that this isn't about the laundry at all. This is about the photos in her phone that she scrolled through in the bathroom. This is about Hendrick's diminishing grins, the loss of his double thumbs-up. He's lost bits and pieces of himself over the years, and maybe Imani let that happen somehow. Maybe her mother was always right about her after all. She pushes away the thought.

Once she finishes collecting all the dirty clothes from the bedrooms, she feels like Santa dragging the bulging laundry bag down the stairs.

"Good Tide-ings," she whispers to herself.

In the downstairs bathroom, she finds a *Looney Tunes* nightgown resting on the pile of laundry in the corner. Sometimes, Hendrick will shower down here when she's using the shower upstairs, but this isn't Hendrick's. This doesn't belong to either of the children. When she touches the grimy nightshirt, goosebumps surge up and down her arm. Her head trembles lightly. After a moment, she recalls purchasing the nightshirt herself during a late-night online shopping binge. She snickers at her own paranoia and tosses the *Space Jam* shirt in the Santa bag. A cloud of uneasiness follows her out of the bathroom, through the living room, down the basement stairs. By the time she reaches the washing machine, she can't remember what it is she's worrying about. Story of her fucking life.

## Tomas

Kennedy's the one who stood on the couch and leaped over the ottoman and almost stumbled into the TV, and yet their mom says, "Outside, you two. And don't come back until you get your ringle-dingles out."

On the neatly trimmed lawn, Kennedy kicks her flip-flop as high into the air as possible and manages to catch the shoe with her bare hands. Tomas can't help but smile, even though he's still upset at his sister for dooming the two of them here. In truth, Tomas doesn't have a single ringle-dingle to expel from his body. All he wants is to spend a nice quiet morning playing the last level of *Goat Flyer* so he can finally eat the Big Bad Can.

"What about bocce ball?" Kennedy says, kicking her flip-flop again. This time, she almost loses her shoe over the brick wall.

"Yeah," Tomas says, rushing over to the side of the lawn. He carefully aligns his feet so that he's standing exactly behind the boundary line. Kennedy brings over the azure bag and lets him throw the little white ball first. A few months ago, Tomas drew a terror-stricken pineapple face on the ball in permanent marker, and thankfully the fruit hasn't lost his luster.

As usual, Kennedy throws all her balls overhand, as hard as she can. On her second turn, she manages to knock the white ball off the lawn.

"Poor pineapple," Kennedy says. "Lost in the abyss for all of time."

While his sister retrieves the white ball, Tomas follows a metallic-looking hummingbird on a zigzagging path from his mom's gnome collection to the raised garden beds that always remind him of coffins, and then over the roof. Facing the house, Tomas notices Marvin watching them from the second-story window. The man waves, but the boy doesn't wave back. For a few seconds, he can't seem to move at all.

Tomas isn't quite sure why he's feeling like such a frightened pineapple, because he liked Marvin when they first met him in Sequoia last summer. Back then, with red-orange flames reflected in his eyes, Marvin told a story about a boy who befriends a ghost wolf and together they stop an evil mime from burning the forest. Marvin said that the mime's famous catchphrase is " ..." When the boy and the wolf fuse together, the boy's eyes burn white, like little full moons.

In spite of all of this, Tomas turns away from Marvin now and takes a few steps away from the house for good measure.

"Wanna go to the tunnel?" Tomas says.

"I think I'm gonna trampoline."

After dropping his neon-yellow bocce ball on the grass, Tomas hops across the stepping-stones imprinted with tiny hands and feet. He goes out of his way to step on his own footprints, to obscure them completely with his black Nikes. He feels a sense of tepid fascination, thinking about himself the size of a baby, but the sentiment only lasts a moment.

To enter the tunnel requires you to climb onto the squat brick wall the back fence rests on. You need to reach high so that you can grip the top of the posts and then walk sideways. Only the front half of your feet can fit on the wall, so you need to walk slowly, carefully. If you happen to slip and fall, you'd better hope there isn't a yard gnome right below you. Their pointy hats can be major deathtraps. Once you reach the corner of the yard, where the two fences almost touch, you squeeze your body through a narrow gap in the corner. Here, you can either jump off the wall onto the dirt or sit first and scoot yourself off. Tomas prefers the scooting method. The tunnel itself is a narrow pathway of dirt and weeds that exists between two fences. Tomas isn't quite sure why this rift exists, and Kennedy wasn't any help when he asked her.

Months ago, he and his sister buried butter knives throughout the tunnel, their blades facing up toward the sky. The two of them memorized the exact location of each knife so that there wasn't any danger of them getting hurt. He tried to explain this to his mom once she figured out about the booby traps, but she made them return everything anyway. At least his mom didn't notice the two-foot-deep hole carpeted with spiky seed pods, covered with sticks and leaves. Tomas wanted to leave a sign on the leaves that read DON'T STEP HERE, because of reverse psychology, but Kennedy convinced him that this probably wouldn't work.

Taking a breath, Tomas steps gingerly over the pit, almost in slow motion. Two crows scream at each other from above, and the boy wonders what exactly they have to argue about. They can fly anywhere in the world. See anything. If Tomas could fly, he would never complain about anything ever again.

As he continues his journey, Tomas keeps his eye out for the glimmer of a knife, just in case they missed one before. He doesn't understand why Kennedy is so obsessed with the trampoline that she won't come here anymore.

At the end of the tunnel, there's a craggy chunk of cement buried partway in the ground that reminds Tomas of a giant's tooth. A giant with bad hygiene. Once, he considered excavating the incisor, but ultimately, he didn't want to waste a good obstruction in the trail. Once you step over this final hurdle, you enter the courtyard. Here, trees of various kinds peek over the fences from all sides and drop their leaves. No one ever rakes this place, so Tomas steps onto a crunchy, spongy floor of scarlet and russet and golden bronze. The courtyard is smaller than Tomas's room, but he still has space enough to sit down and play.

This time, before Tomas even has time to sit, his knees give way and he falls forward onto the soft layer of leaves. He isn't hurt, but the fall startles him. He sits cross-legged on the vegetation, and the fence posts whirl around him. When he lies flat on his back, he feels as if he's rising higher and higher into the indigo sky. He feels light-headed. Almost giddy. When the sensation ebbs, he stays looking up at the sky for a while. Little marshmallows of cloud dash from left to right, while a medical helicopter zooms from right to left.

Tomas can hear the everyone-speaking-at-once rumbling of a barbecue or party. Nevertheless, he experiences an almost tactile sense of solitude. The fences are tall, and the trees surround him and protect him like guardian spirits. The courtyard itself can only be accessed by his own secret path.

Alone, Tomas pulls a few of his main heroes from his jacket pocket. There's the bodybuilding mouse and the headless bobblehead and the army man who only fears balloons. The team easily defeats an invisible croc-topus, but when he wants to play the boy and the wolf spirit, he can't remember the story. He grasps only bits and pieces. The mime's motto is " . . ." When the boy and the wolf come together, his eyes glow like light bulbs. But what else happened?

Ordinarily, Tomas can close his eyes and think back on a happy moment and see everything like he's watching a video game. Right now, he focuses on the campfire. He sees the dancing red-orange flames, the peanut butter cup s'mores, the spark that drifts onto his arm but doesn't burn. At first, Tomas doesn't see Marvin at all, but then the man's head appears, floating next to his mom. His cheeks inflate a little. He doesn't speak, but his mouth opens wider and wider. Too wide.

Tomas collects his heroes as quickly as he can and

rushes through the tunnel, stepping on the edge of the pitfall. Thankfully, he doesn't fall. Once he returns to the world outside, he finds his sister on the lawn again, trying to balance on a bocce ball with one foot. With one look, she hurries over to him.

"What's wrong?" she says.

Only now does Tomas feel the tears on his cheeks. He's not sure why he's crying. He played wolf boy in the courtyard and he came back.

"Nothing," the boy says, wiping his face with a sleeve.

While trying his hand (or foot) at the bocce ball balancing act, he notices some movement in his peripheral vision. When he looks up, Marvin waves at him from the second-story window. Tomas hesitates for a moment and then waves back.

## Hendrick

Hendrick knows full well that his friend is sick as all hell, but that doesn't stop him from sitting on the edge of Marvin's bed and breathing in the virulent air. Even the pyramid of used tissues on the blanket doesn't bother him any. To be honest, Hendrick prides himself on his hearty constitution, his hardy genes. Marvin's flu is just another opportunity to stare suffering in the face and come away unscathed.

"You look like shit," Hendrick says.

"That's fitting, right?" Marvin says, and flicks his nail absentmindedly against an empty bottle of Gatorade. "I mean, I am the new face of diarrhea, nationwide. Did you see the commercial?"

"Yeah, man. It's good. Funny."

The actor shrugs almost imperceptibly. "Good or not, at least I'm living the big life now. I have diarrhea money. I can finally afford Cheesecake Factory."

Hendrick laughs, but as far as he's concerned, this diarrhea commercial is no joke. You have to respect a guy like Marvin who's willing to drop everything in his damn life to make a go at Hollywood. That takes balls, especially for some office peon with wide-set eyes and a nose like Gargamel. Marvin will never be a Channing Tatum or even a Nicolas Cage. Maybe one day, though, he'll be one of those character actors who look more like the caricatures of famous people.

"How's everything at work?" Marvin says, flicking his fucking Gatorade again. This time with two fingers. "Same shitshow? Same cast of mediocre characters?"

"Same everything."

Back when the two of them slogged through the drudgery together, Marvin used to say their workplace was *The Office* if it were produced in hell. That's still as true as ever. Edgar's an incompetent ass who gets half-drunk every lunch and won't stop fiddling with his belt whenever he's chatting with a woman. Brett won't stop lecturing people about factory farms and the dangers of high-fructose corn syrup. Marcella can't take a fucking joke.

"Hey, can you get me one of those?" Marvin points a pinky at the line of bottles on the windowsill. "If I move, I might explode."

Hendrick definitely gets enough do-this-do-that at work, but the poor guy's face looks like a sweaty, bruised peach. How can he say no to a face like that? When Hendrick crosses the room, he notices for the first time all the empty bottles strewn about on the floor. A fiery flash of animosity heats up his forehead, but the feeling dies out as quickly as it came. The moment he grabs a red bottle from off the windowsill, Marvin says, "Could I have the Glacier Freeze? I like to save the Fruit Punch for the end. They're my favorite."

Out of a vague tingling of resentment for having to exchange the red bottle for a blue, Hendrick tosses the Gatorade across the room instead of handing it over. Hendrick doesn't want to hit Marvin in the face, or anything that extreme. But if Marvin isn't able to catch the bottle, Hendrick will be able to chuckle a little and say, "Nice one." In the end, Marvin catches the bottle without even looking in Hendrick's direction.

Gradually, the actor slides his body from a sitting position to where he's flat on his back. He holds the bottle high up above his bed, with his right arm outstretched. Then he tips the Gatorade slightly so that the Glacier Freeze waterfalls into his open mouth.

"What the fuck, man?" Hendrick says. "You're going to choke yourself."

"Oh." Marvin sets the bottle carefully on his stomach. "Right." Then, in a way that makes Hendrick clench his jaw, his friend inches his way back up to a sitting position, shifting his body in small, awkward jerks. Marvin's a great guy and all, but he's certainly as annoying as all hell sometimes. Hendrick enjoys the company of irritating guys, for the most part, but only when they're trying to be.

While Marvin grunts softly in bed, Hendrick takes this opportunity to collect the trash beside the bed. There's little he despises more than picking up after another person, or even himself if truth be told. He moves the small wastepaper basket to a spot on the nightstand so that maybe Marvin won't make another mess.

Once he's sitting up again, the actor says, "Hey, so I did end up watching *Howard the Duck* and there is a duck with boobs in it. I don't know why a duck would have boobs when they're not mammals, but I guess that's what they mean by poetic license, right?"

A dim feeling of déjà vu lights up his mind for a moment. In truth, they probably had dozens of conversations exactly like this, back in the office.

Marvin gulps down some more of that damned Gatorade. "Oh, yeah. I was going to ask. When I was watching *Howard*, I remembered this old animated short. From the Betty Boop era, maybe. So, there's this duck who gets shot in the face by a hunter or a policeman, and his bill shatters to dust. The duck tries on different objects to see if any of them could replace the bill. He tries pinecones and cattails and this pair of knives that he finds in this abandoned car. I think there was blood on the windshield. So, the duck approaches this badger who's his best friend, and the knives slide right into his chest. When the duck tries to talk, the knives move up and down, and the badger's organs spill right out of there. Some of the guts go into the duck's mouth. The problem is, I can't quite remember if this is an actual short I saw, or if it's something else. Does it seem familiar to you at all?"

"No, not really." By now, Hendrick's feeling a small knot of pain in the back of his skull. He can't be sick, though. He never gets sick. "I don't think anyone would make a short like that back in the thirties."

"Yeah. You're probably right."

Right when Hendrick's about to say something like, "Yell if you need anything," his old coworker tosses the now-empty bottle over the side of the bed. The half-hearted little *clunk* of plastic hitting two-year-old hardwood saturates Hendrick's senses.

"You know, I think the duck was wearing a little top hat, now that I think about it."

Outside the guest room, Hendrick wonders what he ever saw in Marvin in the first place. But that's the way with friends, isn't it? Their presence in your life can feel a bit like an anomaly, and you have to wonder what exactly is bonding the two of you together. Heading down the stairs, Hendrick decides that he's in the mood for some Peanut Butter Apocalypse ice cream. Of course, what he really wants is to get out of the house for a while, alone. He wants to hear Morgaine's voice again. He wants her to sever those small cords that connect him to this world. All of this will only be possible if he can manage to get out of the house alone. That's easier said than done, usually.

At the bottom of the stairs, Hendrick stands with his hand in his pocket, fondling his keys. He's only thirty-nine years old, but he experiences another one of those damned brain farts. What exactly is he doing right now? The answer doesn't come, so he settles down in his recliner and plays one of those fireplace videos that Brett introduced him to. Or was it Marvin? The flames in this video burn a dark gray-blue, which is supposed to be especially calming or some such bullshit. Honestly, Hendrick does feel especially calm after a while. He reads the same shitty paragraph in the same shitty book a few times until he rests the book, pages down, on his lap. He knows he should really go upstairs and check on Marvin, but Hendrick's eyes are already closed. The firewood crackles and snaps, and in his sleep, the sounds become voices. "Tsh ks kssss," they say, swarming around his head like invisible bees. They sound urgent, but Hendrick tells them to shut the fuck up. He tells them if they don't speak English, they don't belong here. Finally, the voices buzz off, and Hendrick searches the shadows for a familiar face.

What he does is plunge his hand into a patch of darkness and then swirl his hand around until he feels a strand of hair or the tip of a nose. Once he grabs hold, he has to pull fairly hard in order to get the head out. He's hoping for Morgaine, or someone who looks a little like her at least. Every time he pulls, the faces come out wrong. They're jumbled and knotted and translucent. He almost wishes the swarm of voices would come back, but he is without friends when the veiny faces press deep into his chest and begin to speak.

## Kennedy

Once in a blue moon (or a Smurf moon, as her mom calls it), Kennedy likes to visit one of those websites where you're paired with a random person from around the world in a private chatroom. Most people are either extraordinary perverts or as boring as Kennedy's geometry teacher, Mr. Sizemore. Kennedy will sometimes chat with her teachers before class a little, and Mr. Sizemore's probably the worst teacher to talk to in the universe. "Do you like teaching?" "It's a job. I'm lucky to have one." "Do you have any hobbies?" "Not really." "What's your favorite shape?" "Please go to your seat, Ms. Lund. I need to finish this." On her travels across the internet, Kennedy has encountered countless Mr. Sizemores who don't even ask questions back, and who might as well be trumpet-talking like the adults in Charlie Brown.

The good thing about the random chat website is that every once in a while, you'll jabber with a guy who insists he's a time traveler from the year 4587 or a girl from a country you've never heard of before who doesn't mind sharing what she ate for breakfast.

On the website, you're allowed to set a default for all the strangers, so this time around, she sets the name as Sparkle Fantastico. One of the best Sparkle Fantasticos of the afternoon tells her that Donald Trump is a horseman of the apocalypse. He says Trump's organs are weapons from every time period in human history. A subcompact semiauto .380 ACP for a spleen. A pair of hira shuriken for kidneys. An obsidian blade, crafted by Beelzebub himself, for a heart. Sparkle also says that Rosie O'Donnell is an archangel who can fling Koosh balls made of pure light energy. Kennedy doesn't understand half of what this guy's saying, but she appreciates the overall concept.

After tossing aside a few more extraordinary perverts, Kennedy comes across another worthwhile Sparkle who only eats dinosaur-shaped chicken nuggets. About five years ago, this Sparkle's pet ferret died, and ever since then, every food in the world makes her nauseous except for dinosaur-shaped chicken nuggets. Kennedy can't tell if the woman is telling the truth or not, but she doesn't really mind either way. According to Ms. Fantastico, her ferret Matilda was her sister in a past life, back when the two of them worked in a millinery shop in Paris.

"Sometimes at night, when everyone else is asleep, I can see Matilda's face in the ceiling. I can see her as she was when she was a person. The weird thing is, the two Matildas, the ferret and the human, have similar features. The same dark, round eyes. Their resting faces were both a little frowny-looking, but not an angry frown."

Kennedy pictures two ferrets in straw bonnets decorated with pale pink peonies. Dressed in lavender afternoon dresses, the two sisters smile down at an urchin in suspenders who's trying to sell ferret-faced cupids from a woven basket. Kennedy saw a painting like this somewhere before, only there the people had human faces.

When Ms. Fantastico asks for her favorite memory, Kennedy bristles internally. She's not about to hand over her most precious moments to a second-rate Sparkle Fantastico. Instead, she decides to give Sparkle her third- or fourth-best memory and pretend that it is her most precious.

"So, this was a few years ago, when I was like ten. Me and my family were on our way to some campsite in the desert. Our RV broke down and we had to wait outside by this burned tree. It was about five hundred degrees outside, and we kept waiting for my dad to fix the engine, but he's pretty bad at fixing cars.

"Eventually, my brother sort of wandered off around the tree, and when we found him, he was playing with this dead coyote. My mom washed his hands like a million times, and my brother cried because she wouldn't let him play with the coyote anymore.

"My mom kept telling my dad to call Triple-A, and he finally did after about eighteen hours of yelling at the engine. Me and my brother got pretty bored, so Uncle Marvin took us across this field to these little shops that looked kind of like the Old West. When we were walking across the field, Tomas kept looking everywhere for more dead coyotes. He didn't say that's what he was looking for, but I could tell.

"When we got to those shops, Uncle Marvin bought us some crocodile and kangaroo jerky. I only ate the crocodile jerky because I was pretty into Winnie the Pooh at the time, and I didn't want to eat Roo. In one of the shops, there was this part where you could pay a couple dollars and see all the greatest mysteries of the world. The doorway looked like a big mouth, so Tomas was pretty freaked out to go back there, but Uncle Marvin said he would carry him the whole time.

"The mouth breathed hot air on us when we walked through the doorway. The room was dark and there was a fog machine pumping fog everywhere. It smelled really sweet and chemical-ish. In the room, we saw jars full of dead baby aliens and a mummified cat and a big walnut that grew a human mouth. I don't actually remember all this stuff, but I asked Tomas about it recently and he could describe everything on every shelf.

"I do remember the next room pretty well. We had to walk through this beaded curtain thing, where all the beads were little neon skulls. They made the room look like a kelp forest, with fake kelp hanging from the ceiling. There was even more fog here than the other room, and there was a strong cabbage smell wherever we went. The kelp created a sort of maze that we had to navigate. Sometimes, we had to duck under glowing jellyfish or dried-up piranhas. Tomas still wouldn't walk, even though he liked the fish and everything.

"Finally, we made it all the way through the maze to an open area with piles of bones on the floor. Fish bones and human bones and some of those big shark jaws with the teeth still attached. Near all the bones, there was a mermaid hovering above the floor. There were probably wires or something holding her up, but I didn't see any. She wasn't an Ariel sort of mermaid. Her tail was sharp and spiny, and her face was like one of those deep-sea fish with white eyes and a giant mouth full of needles. An antennae thing dangled from her forehead with a light at the end of it. As soon as we walked in the room, she reached out at us with these webbed claws, her arms all draped with seaweed.

"Uncle Marvin read this plaque on the wall that said you're supposed to put your hand in her mouth and make a wish. If she doesn't bite down and eat your hand, your wish will come true. Tomas cried a little bit, so Uncle Marvin had to carry him back into the kelp area. I knew the mermaid wouldn't eat my hand, but I was still sort of scared. When I walked up onto this raised platform thing, her eyes moved so that she was looking right at me.

I knew the mermaid was fake, but I kept thinking, *Don't bite don't bite don't bite.* I made a wish inside my head and the mermaid did start to bite down a little but not all the way. My hand brushed against her teeth when I was pulling it out but the teeth weren't actually sharp at all. They were foam or something. Tomas said he could hear me scream from where he was. I don't remember screaming at all.

"Tomas kept asking me what I wished for, but I wouldn't tell because that would destroy the wish. In the next store over, Uncle Marvin offered to buy us some ice cream. Neither of us asked for ice cream and we didn't even know there was ice cream in there before Uncle Marvin said that. The weird thing is that's what I asked the mermaid for. Ice cream."

Ms. Fantastico thanks her for the story and before she can ask any follow-up questions, Kennedy says that she needs to go. The teenager types *Fart* and exits the chatroom. She always ends all her online conversations with *Fart.*

When Kennedy told Alejandra the story a few weeks ago, Aly said that the mermaid was probably made of papier-mâché and was probably held up by thin black wires. Kennedy knows this already. The whole reason she likes telling the story is that even a fake mermaid, devoid of magic, can manage to grant a wish every once in a while. No one ever seems to understand that.

Kennedy closes her laptop with a curled pinky and then tilts back in her office chair. Placing her bare feet on her desk, she leans back even farther and searches the ceiling for the face of her own past-life sister. Maybe her sister is a penguin now, or a Parisian street urchin selling miniature mermaid statues.

Unable to find anyone but a daddy longlegs in the ceiling, she lets herself fall backward onto the mound of pillows and blankets behind her. The mountain of softness protects her for the most part, though her neck feels somewhat achy after the plunge. From here, she rolls over onto all fours and crawls over to the plaid backpack that always brings to mind a lumberjack's shirt. This is Saturday, and while she feels an almost moral obligation not to do any homework tonight, she removes *The Witch of Blackbird Pond* from her bag. So far, Hannah Tupper hasn't made anyone's face melt off, but Kennedy is still hopeful. In her backpack, she also spots the single unused cigarette that she discovered in her desk in Ms. Vasquez's class. She almost raised her hand to tell Ms. Vasquez about what she found, but she changed her mind.

Inside her desk the girl keeps a partially crushed matchbox within an old *Blue's Clues* pencil case. The front of the matchbox shows a wide blue eye on a dark blue background. Kennedy feels as if she's seen an eye exactly like this before, possibly inside the room with the dead baby aliens and the big walnut that grew a human mouth. Standing with her back against her bedroom door, she thinks, *No one knock no one knock no one knock.* About a year ago, she dreamed she smoked a cigarette in a cartoonish-looking version of their living room while her mother screamed at her. Sometimes her mother yelled words, and sometimes she shrieked like Fred from *Fred: The Movie.* When Kennedy smoked the dream cigarette, a serpent of fire heated up her tongue and squirmed down her throat into her stomach.

In the present, she lights a match and then quickly picks up the cigarette from off the floor. Her heart runs forward and slams against her chest, over and over, like a football player practicing against one of those foam blocking dummies. She holds the cigarette out in front of her, between two fingers. The flame kisses the paper. A moment passes before she changes her mind and blows out the match like a birthday candle. She even makes a small match-sized wish as the flame dies. The cigarette appears unlit, but she's worried that there's a smoldering spark lurking within the tunnel, waiting to burn her house down. Better safe than sorry, so she stubs out the cigarette on the stone Easter Island head on her desk and then inserts the contraband into a half-drunk bottle of flat Sunkist.

"Sorry," she says, to the Easter Island head. She checks the top of his head for burns, but he seems perfectly fine.

At this point, Kennedy feels less like reading about witches and more like casting her own unearthly hexes. She doesn't know the first thing about witchcraft, so she decides to trampoline instead. Before she can even reach the top of the stairs, Uncle Marvin calls her into his room and asks her for a favor. Apparently, he's starting another one of his weird art projects.

Lying flat on his back, with a bottle balanced on his stomach, Marvin says, "Seriously, only give me the ones you don't care about. I can make do with whatever you don't mind sacrificing to the craft gods."

"Okay," Kennedy says. "What are you using them for?"

"You'll see."

Right when she turns away, he adds, "Oh, and there's a visit to the Ice Scream Factory in this for you. Or 31 Flavors. Wherever you want."

Back in her bedroom, Kennedy drags army-green storage boxes from the darkest depths below her bed. For some cryptic reason, the insides of the boxes smell like old books, though there's nothing here but old toys and a few penguin print T-shirts much too small for her to wear anymore. People in her elementary school used to call her Penguin, or Pengy, but those days are long gone.

Slowly, Kennedy constructs a wall of dolls across her floor, using the extra doll clothes as a sort of mortar. The image reminds her of those catacombs from Paris, with all the tunnels made of skulls and bones. She read online that the reason they started the catacombs was because there were so many open graves and unearthed corpses, people wouldn't stop complaining about the smell. Sometimes, a cemetery would burst under a heavy shower of rain, and rotting bodies would spew out onto people's private property. Ultimately, Kennedy decides to re-form the wall into a more tranquil-looking mountain of figures.

The trick to deciding which doll clothes should be kept and which should be sacrificed is to rub each outfit between two fingertips and wait. Her heart either whirls inside her, like a flurry of autumn leaves, or it doesn't. Sometimes, she needs to imagine herself on the edge of a jagged cliff, tossing the chiffon maxi dress (or whatever she's holding at the moment) into the grasping, claw-like waves below. The dress shrivels and sinks deeper and deeper, toward the deep-sea mermaids with ashen eyes and cadaverous faces. Does the thought make her want to cry or not?

In truth, Kennedy doesn't want to get rid of any of

her doll clothes, in the same way that she doesn't throw away her movie stubs or her old school notebooks. At the same time, she wants to make Uncle Marvin happy. He may not be a blood uncle, but he's been a part of her life since she was five or six. Whether she's performing the *Totoro* theme song on her saxophone, or reading a poem she wrote about wild dogs living in the ruins of Pompeii, Uncle Marvin's always there to give her that stupid double thumbs-up. Kennedy's dad used to give her that same double thumbs-up years ago, when she was very young. She's not sure whether Uncle Marvin learned the move from her dad, or if it was the other way around.

In the end, Kennedy dumps a hefty double handful of miniscule clothes and accessories onto Marvin's bed. Somehow, she manages all this without a single tear, or even an echo of a tear.

"Yeah, these will work," Uncle Marvin says, lifting a monarch butterfly–style fairy gown with his pinky. "We'll go to that ice cream place as soon as I'm feeling better. I'm still a regular Sicky Vicky, or Heavin' Steven. Those are Garbage Pail Kids. Probably before your time."

Kennedy's tempted to ask him again what he's planning on doing with all the clothes, but he won't tell her, she's sure. Uncle Marvin likes surprises.

Before she leaves, he gives her a double thumbs-up and says, "Don't leave me hanging." So she gives him a double thumbs-down back.

"Agh, that hurts," he says, with a hand over his heart.

In her bedroom, as the girl returns her toys to the plastic storage boxes, she pictures a wall of doll heads crumbling apart. Ferret corpses gush from the cracks, dressed in straw bonnets and afternoon dresses. Maybe she'll write a poem about a wall of dolls someday, but for now she pushes the image from her mind. With her palms, she brushes down the goosebumps on her arms.

Instead of storing away the tiny stovepipe hat from her keep pile, she decides to place it on the Easter Island head. He deserves a little luxury, after the day he's had. After she slides the storage boxes to the darkest depths of her room, she returns to the land of Sparkle Fantasticos. She types, alone in her room, searching once again for astrophysicists and Nigerian grandmothers and ventriloquist dummies brought to life by dark magicks. From the words of these strangers, she sees that the world is filled with beauty and with horrors, and she's not quite sure which she likes hearing about more.

## Imani

Using her husband's hand pruners, Imani slices slowly through the peeling, brambly flesh of the rosebush. She squeezes the handle again and again, until the dull blade eats completely through the base. As soon as the bush collapses, hundreds of shriveled leaves jostle loose and flutter to the ground, like a swarm of insects all dying at once.

Hendrick noticed the first dead bush months ago. He said gophers had likely eaten the roots. He said he would go to Home Depot the next day. His exact words were: *The damned dirty rodents are as good as dead.*

Now Imani cuts her way through a second dead bush, and then a third. Only the last bush in the row remains alive. In her mind, she promises the plant that she'll buy the gopher poison soon.

Out loud, to the empty yard, she says, "I'll gopher broke to keep you alive." A crow or raven caws in the distance, but no one else seems to appreciate her pun.

Imani puts on some shabby gardening gloves before stuffing the bushes into the green waste bin, but ultimately, the fabric doesn't provide her much protection. She cringes when a particularly malicious thorn stabs her right where she cut herself the night before.

Right after she accidentally broke her grinning peanut statue, Hendrick said, "I'm sorry." But he didn't seem sorry. Imani wonders if he remembers that he bought her the eyeless peanut when they were first engaged. They found him at the Hamburger Man Thrift Shop, which the two of them named after the giant fiberglass statue at the entrance that no one ever purchased. She remembers the hamburger-headed man held a spatula in one hand and a butcher knife in the other. Hendrick liked to tell her that one day she'd come home and find the thrift shop's mascot on their front porch, staring at her with those sesame seed eyes. When they first laid eyes on the smiling peanut, Hendrick said they found Hamburger Man's long-lost brother.

The throbbing in her finger quells by the time she removes Hendrick's gardening gloves. Her Band-Aid must have caught in the fabric, because she can see her cut, still closed and barely noticeable, despite the thorn's best efforts. Unconsciously, she brings the small wound, which now tastes of lawn clippings and lavender, to her lips.

On her way to the sliding glass door, she steps on what turns out to be a toy mouse with a handlebar mustache. She doesn't have any pockets, so she carries the creature all the way upstairs, into her bedroom, and places him on her nightstand, where he flexes his eight-pack amidst a forest of amber candles. Ordinarily, Imani will spend a couple hours cleaning on a Saturday morning, and then move on to bigger and better things, like true crime podcasts or Lin-Manuel Miranda or hikes through a moderately haunted forest. Today, no matter how much she cleans, she can't seem to satisfy herself. There's a nervous, almost panicky energy in her arms and legs that won't dissipate.

As Imani's folding laundry, Hendrick comes in carrying a toilet paper roll in one hand and his iPad in the other.

"I was going to do that," he says, motioning to the piles of laundry with the toilet paper.

"Then why didn't you?" Imani says, the words spilling out of her in a torrent that sounds angrier than she intended.

"I didn't because you woke up at four in the damn morning and beat me to it. What was I supposed to do? Wake up at three?"

Imani sighs. "You know that's not what I was suggesting. You could have done the laundry days ago. The hampers were overflowing."

"And that's the worst thing in the world, right? Overflowing hampers, dust on a porcelain bird, a lampshade slightly askew."

Imani sets Tomas's Fizzgig shirt on the bed and takes a deep, cinnamon-scented breath through her nose. "Can we quit while we're ahead here? I'm sorry for snapping at you. I'm having a shit day."

"Fine with me." With that, he storms toward the en suite, running into the cedar chest at the foot of the bed. He manages to catch himself before falling on his face.

"Did you move the furniture?" he says.

Imani can't help but laugh a little.

"I'm serious," he says. "The bed seems . . ."

"Babe, what are you talking about?"

"Nothing. Never mind." He inches his way into the bathroom, turning his head left and right. He shuts the door, gently, as if he's too frightened to make a sound. Imani feels the smile sink down her face.

"Babe, are you okay in there?" she says.

"Leave me be, woman," he says, sounding more like his huffy self again. "I'm doing God's work in here."

While folding laundry, Imani scrutinizes the bedroom for any aberrations. Eventually, she inserts her earbuds and continues the episode she started yesterday, about a man who killed only men with blond hair and buried them with their chest cavities full of fertilized chicken eggs.

In a few minutes, she pauses the episode and places the mouse toy on a modest tower of folded laundry. The mouse rests on the slobbering mouth of Slimer.

Setting the laundry on the floor, Imani uses the family knock on Tomas's half-open door. For a moment, she remembers her own mother removing the screws from the door hinges. She remembers her mother grunting as she dragged Imani's bedroom door away. This was a punishment, for some small sin she doesn't remember anymore.

"Special delivery," Imani says, setting the clothes on Tomas's bed.

Tomas pauses his computer game and spins around in his chair. He's not usually a kid who looks a person in the eyes, but right now he studies her face, a sharp-edged look of concern dominating his usually soft features.

She holds out the mouse toy and says in her best Mickey Mouse impression, "You forgot me outside. I tried to take it in stride. Then I cried."

"Mom, that's not how he talks."

"Okay, how does he talk, then?"

In a hoarse, gremlin-like voice, Tomas says, "Hello."

Imani flies the mouse over to the boy's desk and makes him crash-land next to a family of glow-in-the-dark zombies. The mouse still seems unafraid, even millimeters from a growing, undead bloodhound.

For a time, Imani watches her son play his computer game. On the screen, a caped goat soars through an asteroid field populated with spinning hay bales and demonic carrots. Of course, the mother aims her attention less on the galactic battle and more on the way her son giggles and gasps as he plays, the way he hops out of his chair when the goat explodes in a supernova of guts and half-digested T-shirts.

Eventually, the flying goat faces a titanic tin can wearing a pinstriped fedora and a wispy mustache. Tomas avoids a barrage of exploding peas and asparagus missiles. After a few seconds, though, the poor goat is devoured.

"In Russia, can eats goat," Imani says.

The gigantic tin can takes a bite out of Earth, chuckling as he chews, and Tomas stares at the screen in silence.

"You'll get him," Imani says. "If you get really stuck, you should ask Uncle Marvin. He's good at games, isn't he?"

"Yeah," Tomas says as the goat's body parts surge to the beginning of the level and amalgamate into a hero once again. The goat vomits up a new cape made from a patchwork of fabric scraps.

Returning to her bedroom, Imani finds her husband sitting cross-legged on the bed, watching some mobster movie on his iPad, folding laundry.

He glances up at her and says, "I'm sorry you're having a shitty day. Is there anything going on?"

"No." Part of her wants to tell him that she's feeling overly, nebulously anxious, even by her standards. But if she does reveal this, he'll only suggest that she go on a hike or take a lavender bath or eat some wild-caught salmon.

"Why don't we go to Antony's tonight?" she says. "Marvin can watch the kids."

"Marvin's recovering from surgery," Hendrick says,

folding one of her floral midi skirts in a way that defies all logic and reason. "He can hardly get out of bed. Anyway, we already went to a restaurant this week. What about our once-a-week rule? You wanted to put aside some extra money for Christmas."

"Yeah," Imani says, quietly. "You're right."

Of course, the truth is that Hendrick doesn't want to go to Antony's. If he did, he would suggest that she ask Trinity to come babysit. He would try to convince her that breaking the once-a-week rule isn't the worst thing in the world. He would tell her that Christmas wouldn't be ruined by one date night. But is all this true, or is she projecting her own fears onto him again?

"Maybe we could watch some Netflix later," Imani says.

"Yeah," her husband says, his eyes on a bullet-riddled mobster on his iPad. "Sure."

They continue folding, and Imani delivers a stack of flannel and denim to Kennedy. The girl graces her with a "Thanks, Mom" before returning her attention to her library book, slapping a flip-flop against her heel as she reads.

"How is it?" Imani says.

"Good, but not enough curses. I don't think the woman's even a witch at all."

"Are all the words *spelled* right, at least?"

"Mom, no."

Next, Imani collects a few threadbare T-shirts and stretchy exercise pants from off her bed. She wonders if Marvin brought this surfing Worf shirt at random or as an intentional homage to the past. She didn't know Marvin or Hendrick back in their college days, but she's heard all the stories. She knows the two of them hosted Trek Meets in their dorm's community room, where they watched *The Next Generation* and drank vodka and cranberry juice from Big Gulp cups. Their immeasurable Trekkiness is what initially brought the two of them together.

"Special delivery," she says, out of force of habit.

"Oh, cool," Marvin says, holding an oversized pencil between two fingers, a legal pad on his lap. "My clothes were starting to smell a little like durian fruit."

On her way to the dresser, Imani's legs buckle and the clothing slips from her hands. The blood in her face plummets elsewhere into her body. She takes a seat on the faux leather tub chair in the corner.

"You okay?" Marvin says, repositioning his whole body so that he can face her.

"Just a little dizzy," Imani says. "I probably spent too much time in the sun, hacking at dead things."

"Wow, you sound like a regular zombie hunter." He taps the bulbous pencil eraser against his forehead. "Oh, that reminds me. Do you have *Dead Alive* on Blu-ray? I didn't finish looking through your collection earlier, so I'm not sure what you have Peter Jackson–wise."

"Sorry, I don't remember ever seeing that."

"That's a shame." Marvin attempts, unsuccessfully, to spin the large pencil in his hand. "There's this zombie baby named Selwyn who really steals the show. At one point, the main guy takes Selwyn to the park, and the baby gets launched into the sky using a teeter-totter. I read somewhere that Jackson finished the movie under budget, so he used the extra money to shoot that park scene. It's a great scene."

"Sounds like it."

Throughout this conversation, her disequilibrium fades, only to be replaced with a piercing headache behind her eyes. She can feel her heartbeat pulsing in the veins of her neck, and also in the cut on her finger. With a pang in her stomach, she wonders if she's getting ill, with a cold or flu or worse. But she can't recall any other symptoms. She's felt unusually sprightly the last few days, hasn't she? No headaches before this one, no stomach problems, nothing to complain about at all.

Taking a deep breath, Imani stands and feels steady on her feet, thankfully.

"Feeling better?" Marvin says, scribbling on his yellow pad.

"Much."

"Good good good."

As she puts away Marvin's clean clothes, she sees the man's reflection in the streaky mirror above the dresser. Was she supposed to clean the mirror before Marvin arrived, or was Hendrick? In the reflection, Marvin sniffs at the air and wrinkles his nose.

When she turns to face the real Marvin, he says, "I finished writing up those measurements for that project I told you about. The clothes don't need to be perfectly tailored or anything, so don't worry too much. You sure you don't mind helping me out?"

"Of course not," Imani says.

"Kennedy gave us some old doll clothes and such to work with." He points to the kaleidoscopic mound of fabric with the broken point of his pencil. She wonders for a moment if he has an oversized sharpener that could reform the point, or if he has to use a knife.

Marvin hands her the whole legal pad and says, "Once I can get out of bed easier, we should watch *Dead Alive*. It's funny. You would like it."

"Sounds like a plan," Imani says.

He tries again to swirl the pencil in his fingers and the eraser ends up hitting him on the side of his head. "Agh."

Instead of going straight to her bedroom with the miniature clothes, she decides to check with Kennedy first and make sure she's okay with all of this. After all, this doesn't sound like Kennedy at all. The last time they had a yard sale, her daughter cried at the mere suggestion that she get rid of a few dolls and penguins.

"Yeah, Uncle Marvin can use those," Kennedy says, without even a tremor in her voice. "They're not important ones."

"Are you sure?"

"Mom, I said yeah."

At least somewhat satisfied, Imani heads back into the hallway and suddenly remembers that Marvin despises the smell of cinnamon. That's why he was wrinkling his nose before. She carefully uses her big toe to switch off the plug-in air freshener. They'll need to change over to a different scent while Marvin's staying here. Do they make Gatorade-scented air fresheners? She smiles at the thought.

In the bedroom, she finds Hendrick curled up on his side, snoring in that gentle way that makes him sound as if he's wheezing. Ordinarily, her husband sleeps on his stomach with his arm under the pillow, so he looks unnatural and childlike in this position. An earbud still dangles from one ear. On the iPad screen, a woman in red smashes a glass bottle on a gravestone.

"No," he whispers, in a frail voice that doesn't sound like his own. He rolls over and faces the other way. "The heads."

On her sewing table, Imani dumps out the tattered plastic bag that Marvin supplied her. She sorts the doll clothes into heaps of dresses, tops, pants, and accessories. She studies Marvin's legal pad, and the handwriting appears quivery and disproportioned, probably because of his recent surgery. He is on heavy painkillers, after all.

"How long was I asleep?" Hendrick says, his catchphrase whenever he wakes up from a nap.

"Not long," Imani says.

She could turn around and ask if he wants to watch one of their shows on Netflix, but she doesn't want to hear another halfhearted "Yeah, sure." Instead, she begins dismembering the doll clothes with her seam ripper and her titanium micro-tip scissors. Gradually, everything comes to pieces. For a while, she thinks about their first house, where Kennedy would use all her strength to yank open the bottom freezer drawer of their fridge. Then she would bury as many dolls as possible in the massive ice tray. "They're so cold," she would say. "They're shivering."

In time, Imani begins reconstructing the clothes based on Marvin's specifications. He hasn't supplied her with sewing patterns in any sense, but she does the best she can, using his overall concepts and measurements. Hours pass as she cuts and sews and embroiders teensy sections of felt. The longer she works, the more unrecognizable the doll clothes become.

Only when she pricks her finger with an embroidery needle does she notice her forehead aching, an invisible hand pressing hard against her skull from within. For a moment, she worries she might be getting sick, but then again, she's felt perfectly healthy all day. She's probably fine.

## *Tomas*

Tomas turns to Google Images because he doesn't recognize half the objects Uncle Marvin scribbled on this piece of yellow notebook paper. On the bullet list, there's a potbelly stove, a dress form, an industrial sewing machine table, a curved garment rack. The boy doesn't understand why his uncle would ask him to contribute to one of his projects, but he jumps at the opportunity nevertheless.

"Don't worry about making everything perfect," Uncle Marvin told him, minutes ago. "And feel free to put your own stamp on things. I can work with whatever you give me."

Tomas doesn't know what Uncle Marvin means by *stamp,* but he spends a good minute or two staring at potbelly stoves on his computer screen, allowing the images to burrow deep inside his mind. Once he feels satisfied with the transference, he sits cross-legged on his giant squid rug and gets to work. He uses his most special pens, with color names like coquelicot and fulvous and sorrel.

Despite holding his breath as much as possible for good luck, Tomas can't get the potbelly stove quite right. In one drawing, the stove looks too melancholy. In another, he seems like there's not a spark of life in him at all. The boy can feel the tears climbing up the inside of his face, trying to jump out. He takes a deep breath. Sometimes, when he's feeling especially frustrated at his drawings, he takes himself back in time to when he visited his uncle's apartment for the first time. He can't remember everything from when he was three or four, but he can recall every moment of this outing.

Tomas recollects a papier-mâché T. rex standing beside an empty coat stand, wearing a mustard turtleneck and crimson sneakers. Taxidermied birds hung from the living room ceiling on strings, a few of them swaying gently in the current of the air conditioning. Christmas lights wrapped around the legs of the coffee table like robotic snakes. And bright watercolor paintings covered an entire wall. Paintings of goblins dressed in burlap sacks and a duck playing an electric guitar and a translucent creature with rose-colored dots for eyes.

"We can leave if you want to," his mother kept saying,

squeezing his hand a little too hard.

Uncle Marvin led them over to the dining room, where he stood on a chair so that he could see. On the table stood a pint-sized park, frozen in time. Zombie babies made from painted clay shrieked with delight on a teeter-totter. The duck from the painting in the living room careened down a spiraling slide while playing his electric guitar with his bill. Bordering the duck pond grew a toothpick oak tree. Children scrambled up the bare branches as sea serpents rose from the muddy waters of the lily pond and stretched toward the children with open mouths.

"It's just pretend," his mother said, holding his hand as he balanced on the creaking chair. Tomas knew that Uncle Marvin created all this, and he wasn't afraid. That day, his father didn't have to lean close to his ear and tell him to stop crying.

At one point during the visit, Tomas wandered off into the kitchen with his sister, where he found a cerulean marker balanced upright on the floor, right in front of the dishwasher. On the nearest linoleum tile, Tomas quickly drew his own T. rex wearing a cerulean turtleneck and cerulean sneakers.

"Dad!" Kennedy yelled, tossing the marker far away as if it were a grenade ready to explode. "Tomas drew on the ground!"

"Shit," their dad said as soon as he spotted the drawing. "Shit, I hope that wasn't permanent. I'm sorry, Marvin. We'll clean this up."

"Nah, leave it," Uncle Marvin said, crouching down next to the drawing. "I like it."

Tomas didn't say anything to that. He was too frightened his father would yell some more, but the boy remembers wanting to draw on the walls and then shrink himself down to the size of the zombie babies so he could play in the monster park. He wanted to build a giant castle of toothpicks that touched the ceiling, with cat-faced dragons and lumpy demons climbing the walls.

Those feelings churning inside the three-year-old Tomas smash through the memory, somehow, flowing into the Tomas of now like a time-traveling stream of emotion. Tomas can hear his uncle's voice, clear as a magic crystal. "I like it," he said. Tomas's tears give up on trying to get out, and a cheerful potbelly stove emerges from his fingers instead.

While cutting out the drawing, the boy wonders where exactly his artwork will fit in Uncle Marvin's world. Maybe the children in the oak tree will escape at last and find themselves in a creepy attic full of dress forms and sewing tables. Maybe Tomas is furnishing an upside-down house for upside-down people on the ceiling.

He continues drawing objects until he decides to curl up on the rug and rest his eyes. Then he's up again a moment later. Crows wrestle with one another above his head, dropping blood and iridescent feathers on the floor.

"This hardwood is only two years old," Tomas says. He picks up feather after feather, but there doesn't seem to be any end to them.

Dinosaur heads force themselves through cracks in the walls, and the boy realizes this probably isn't his room after all. Scorching tears trickle down his cheeks while he stares at the creature in the painting with bloody droplets for eyes. The dinosaur heads mouth words with their human lips, but Tomas doesn't understand what they're trying to say. His biggest problem though is that no matter where he turns his body, his face swivels toward the painting as if pulled by a magnet.

The creature presses his face against the painting until the glass shatters onto the floor. This is yet another mess someone will have to clean up later. The creature pushes his face through the frame, and suddenly Tomas is watching from above, roosting in the rafters with all the crows.

"Poor guy," Tomas says, watching as the creature wraps his limbs around and around. The boy below opens his mouth but says nothing at all.

## Hendrick

Sometimes, like on nights such as tonight, Hendrick worries that his system is too perilous, too fraught with unnecessary danger. *Buddy, you're a fool,* he thinks to himself, in a voice that sounds a little too much like his father for his taste. When all's said and done, though, Hendrick doesn't want to change his system. He wants to stage-whisper "Banana!" a few times while lying on the gunmetal velvet, to see if his wife will stir. She doesn't. Then he wants to creep down the stairs, avoiding that spot on the second-to-last step that creaks. Using his phone in flashlight mode, he wants to descend into the glacial basement, where he can remove the false bricks from the far wall.

He reaches deep into the gaping maw in the wall, and he imagines the basement biting down and gnawing off his arm. He smiles, even though he doesn't find the thought humorous in the least. He pulls his stack of hundreds from the hole, still thick enough to quicken his pulse.

"Zip-a-dee-doo-dah," he says. He feels himself blushing a moment later. He thought he purged his grandmother's weird expressions from his vocabulary long ago.

No matter; he sits on the plastic storage box in the middle of the floor and places his phone beside him, the beam of light pointed at the menagerie of spiders on the ceiling. He runs his thumb down the stack of bills, again and again. Sometimes, on nights like tonight, he wonders what he would do if the basement door opened and Imani's silhouette stood immobile in the doorway above. "Sweetie," he would say. "There's something I need to show you." What else could he say?

The red rubber band he took from work breaks apart while he attempts to slide it off the hundreds. He tosses the rubber band on the floor, and then thinks better of it. But the instant he pockets the trash, he feels stupid for doing so. What could Imani possibly say? "I found this rubber band in the basement. Is there something you need to tell me, babe?"

Hiccupping suddenly, Hendrick transfers a few bills into his awaiting wallet. He never knows quite how much to add, and every time he sits down here, the amount changes. Tonight, his hand won't seem to stop. He reminds himself that he can't go too crazy with this. Imani would notice a bulging wallet. She notices everything. Finally, his hand stops and he sits there for a while, with his stash in one hand and his wallet in the other. He looks up at the labyrinth of webs above, but he can't spot a single spider. Maybe they're afraid of the light. Hendrick stands from the box.

And then, like a nightmare, the basement door opens,

and the silhouette that appears isn't Imani at all. What Hendrick sees is an emaciated-looking shadow with a bulbous head. Arms like ropes squirm at the shadow's sides.

"Boo," the dark figure grumbles, and the door closes.

Hendrick hiccups again, dropping his money on the floor. The impact doesn't make any sound whatsoever. With his phone in hand, he searches the entire basement for any bill that might have escaped him. His heart still won't calm down, and he chastises his brain for the strange imaginings about the man in the doorway. Why does he do this to himself so often? This can't be good for his blood pressure.

Satisfied that he hasn't left any hundreds behind, Hendrick attempts to tie up the stack with the broken rubber band from his pocket. He only manages to snap the band into more pieces. In the end, he seals up the stack unbound. There isn't any danger to leaving them loose, is there? The bills won't sprout out between the false bricks like some invasive vine.

On his way up the stairs, Hendrick hiccups so violently that he drops his phone. The device tumbles and all his light dissolves in an instant. A rivulet of perspiration runs down his back as he backtracks carefully down the stairs. For some reason, he feels more comfortable walking backward instead of turning around. Once he reaches the bottom, he searches the icy cement floor on all fours, and he remembers his own childhood dog locked alone in a dark garage as punishment for urinating on a wool, hand-knotted rug. He can't find the phone anywhere. Of course his brain betrays him once again, and he pictures the rawboned silhouette staring at him from above. In his mind, he sees the creature hunched forward, slinking down the stairs, its arms squirming at its sides.

He snickers at himself. He's as bad as Tomas. The boy cries without a night-light.

Crawling forward a little farther, Hendrick makes a bizarre yelping sound he's never heard before, because a tiny object pierces his palm. With his other hand, he pulls what feels like a goathead thorn out of his skin. Then he drags himself in what he hopes is the direction of the storage box, because he wants to place the goathead on top. He doesn't want to get stabbed by the thing again. As he moves now, he feels pinpricks of pain moving from the left side of his head to the right. He can't be getting sick. He never gets sick.

Finally, his right hand brushes against what he assumes is his phone. He's right. He of course wanted to use the flashlight to guide his way upstairs, but the screen won't turn on anymore. He should have expected as much from that tumble. Sighing, he pockets the phone and checks to make sure that his wallet's still in his back pocket. Incomprehensibly, his eyes seem to be adjusting to the dark, because he can see a shadowy, amorphous version of the stairs to his right. But how can that be? This place is always pitch black at this time of night. Heading up the stairs, he notices there's a sliver of jaundiced light coming from under the door. Someone's up there. Someone's awake.

Hendrick ascends the stairs, squeezing the handrail as tightly as possible, and for a few seconds his pain becomes a shower of glass shards sprinkling on the top of his brain. A psychedelic laser show dances in front of his eyes. And then the sensation fizzles to nothing.

The pain and colors disturb him, but he'll have to deal with that later. For now, he reaches out and his hand pauses an inch from the doorknob. More cold sweat dribbles down his back. "Sweetie," he'll say. "There's something I need to show you." What else can he do?

Hendrick crosses the threshold, and Imani's not standing on the other side with her arms crossed over her chest. Instead, he finds his brother facing the far wall, with what looks like a backpack under his robe. Hendrick stands there in silence for a while, staring.

"Marv," he says, finally.

His brother turns around, and waves at him with a permanent marker in his hand.

"What are you doing out of bed?" Hendrick says, his voice cracking in the middle of the sentence.

"I'm drawing on all these photos," his brother says. "I can only manage shitty little stick figures, but fine art isn't everything, right? These stick guys are only starting points. Little taps on the mind to say, hey, there's something here."

"What the fuck are you talking about?"

"You're sounding a bit loud. Do you want to wake up the kids? Imani?" Marv sniffs at the tip of the marker and wrinkles his nose.

Stepping closer to the wall, Hendrick sees now that Marv has in fact drawn stick figures on their family photos. His brother's always been eccentric, painting portraits of caterpillars with dog faces and shit like that, but this is next-level bizarre.

"Man, why would you do this?" Hendrick says.

Marvin laughs through his nose, in that annoying way of his. "You're seriously going to act all incredulous about my nighttime activities while you get your rocks off hiding from your wife, crawling around an empty room in the middle of the night? Don't you think that's a little on the pathetic side?"

When Hendrick hiccups this time, his back tenses to the point of pain. An amalgam of shame and anger and fear heats up his forehead and the back of his neck. He wants to rush forward and shake his brother by the shoulders, but he doesn't. They're not five years old anymore.

Marvin sighs. "Hey, I'm sorry. I shouldn't lash out at you like this. You're one of my people. My back's just killing me and my psyche's shattering and you're an easy target."

"Just how high are you right now?" Hendrick says. "Is it your meds or did you bring some recreational shit into my house? Tell me the truth, Marv. I don't want that shit in my house."

Without another word, Marvin drops the marker and heads for the stairs.

"You stay where you fucking are," Hendrick says.

"Keep your voice down," Marvin whispers over his shoulder, still wearing that damned rounded backpack under his robe.

Another headache hits Hendrick, like a hundred goat-heads pushed against the top of his skull. The pain doesn't dissipate this time, so he shuffles to the couch and collapses. His eyes feel as if they're about to erupt. He massages his eyelids with the tips of his fingers. When the pain finally fades, he stands and glances around the room. Imani, or one of the kids perhaps, turned on the stained-glass floor lamp, but they're not here anymore. If Imani's awake upstairs and asks him where he was, he'll tell her he went downstairs for a glass of root beer and he heard a sound coming from the basement. He's not sure exactly what word to use to describe the sound. A knocking? A grumbling? He wants her to take the sound seriously, but at the same time he doesn't want to frighten her so much that she won't fall asleep again. What about a clanking?

Heading for the lamp, Hendrick spots a black marker on the floor with the cap removed. He performs a quick scan of the room, but he doesn't see the cap anywhere. Why someone would leave a permanent marker lying around like this, he can't begin to fathom. He picks up the Sharpie and when he stands, he notices a lopsided picture frame on the wall. He straightens the frame. And for a while, he stares at his wife as she holds Tomas against her chest, the two of them wrapped up in the same fuzzy pink blanket that they brought from home. She won't even look up for a second for the camera. Imani's eyes stay on Tomas, on his weird cone-shaped head. Marvin's off to the side, holding Kennedy up so she can see her new brother. She's reaching out to him with both hands, her fingers spread wide. Marvin's face glows red and yellow and green, reflecting the light of the stained-glass lamp. When Hendrick turns away from the photo, the spots of color remain for a time, floating in his vision, following him wherever he turns. He turns off the light and carries the marker into the upstairs bathroom, where he mummifies the thing in toilet paper and throws it away.

Thankfully, Imani isn't waiting for him on their bed, sitting with her arms crossed over her chest. She's lying on her side, in another world, her eyes quivering behind her lids.

While sitting on the floor, removing his oxfords, Hendrick feels the sudden urge to break from his system. He wants to tell her about the false bricks and the money and maybe even Brett's apartment. That crease will appear between her eyebrows and she'll shoot daggers at him, and swords, and missiles. She probably won't talk to him for a few days, but she'll forgive him, eventually.

But of course the feeling runs dry, the way it always does, and Hendrick climbs slowly into the bed. Imani stirs a little as the bed creaks. For a few moments, Hendrick stays perfectly still, his heartbeat thrashing in his neck. Then he rolls over, facing the darkened photos on the wall, and he lets everything go.

# SUNDAY

## *Kennedy*

Sunday Bunday isn't off to a great start with a fox demon emoji fuming there on Kennedy's phone. It's always a bad sign when Alejandra sends a single emoji without any text. That means she's too pissed off for words.

What's wrong? Kennedy texts back.

And of course, Alejandra doesn't respond all the time Kennedy dresses in her gray leggings and slightly grayer tank top. She doesn't respond while the teenager searches her bookshelf of stuffed animals for that pastel penguin with bunny ears. Kennedy leaves the penguin right outside of Tomas's door and then heads downstairs with her phone balanced on her head. But she abandons the balancing act as soon as the device begins to slip. If she obliterates another phone, her dad's head will probably go supernova.

In the kitchen, she finds her mother sweeping curved shards of emerald glass from off the floor.

"Don't come in without shoes," her mother says, still looking at the floor.

"I'm wearing shoes," Kennedy says.

The girl sits at the table with the rabbit-themed table-cloth. Her mom doesn't always go all out for Sunday Bunday, but today seems to be the exception. Kennedy attempts to balance her phone vertically on the table, on top of a pipe-smoking rabbit in a purple overcoat. Her attention meanders to a little white feather stuck to her mother's cardigan, and then to the speckling of rain outside, too light to even hear.

"You're quiet this morning," her mother says, searching the fridge, the feather quivering on her back.

"I'm practicing my telepathy," Kennedy says. "Listen."

Her mom turns around, holding an egg carton and a tube of cinnamon rolls. "Oh, thanks," she says. "I am the coolest mom in the world, aren't I?"

Kennedy spins her phone on the table. "I read about this guy once who moved into a new house. I think it was in New Hampshire. Somewhere in New England. The first day he stayed there, he kept seeing flashes of red fabric and dirt and roots. He thought maybe the house was reminding him of something from his childhood. Something with dirt. Eventually, though, he started seeing more. He saw hair and skin and muscle. Organs.

"He kept seeing all this every day. He was too freaked out to tell his family or even his boyfriend, who lived nearby. After a couple weeks of this, he got some different flashes, of grass and a red maple tree. This wasn't just any maple tree, either. This was the tree in his backyard.

"The guy didn't have a clue about what was going on, but he went outside in the rain and walked around on his lawn and looked at the tree. He didn't notice anything out of the ordinary. Then he got another flash while he was out there, and this one was of his own tennis shoe. He realized he was seeing himself standing out there on the grass.

"He still felt pretty confused about everything, but he grabbed a shovel and dug a hole in his lawn, right where he was standing when he got the flash of his shoe. When he told this story later, he said that he didn't expect to find anything in the ground, but that he needed to know for sure. He thought he could maybe make the flashes stop if he proved to himself that there was nothing there. So he dug and he dug, and he found a dead woman in a red dress, buried in his yard. He learned later that her name was Margo or Margaret, I think. She was a missing person. She was married with four kids and like a hundred dogs and cats. Her family said she went out for cough medicine, and she never came back.

"So the guy, the guy who moved into the house, thinks that maybe he had a telepathic link with the insects that were eating the woman's body. That's why he could see her organs and everything. He never got any flashes after that, and he never did before he moved into the house, either. It was a one-time thing."

"Wow," her mother says. "Where did you read about that?"

"Online."

While watching her mother crack some eggs, Kennedy tries her hand (or brain) at a little telepathy and projects the words *Text me* into the universe. Tragically, her phone doesn't vibrate a text notification in response.

She wonders if the man-and-the-insects story is actually true. And then she wonders if her dad and Uncle Marv ever know what the other's thinking, the way twins sometimes can on TV. She's never known her dad and uncle to even finish each other's sentences, so maybe fraternal twins don't get those sorts of powers.

Her mother hands over the Pillsbury cinnamon buns so that Kennedy can pop open the tube and relish the little explosion of dough. Since Alejandra still refuses to text a single word, Kennedy abandons the phone on the table and helps her mom with the plates and cups and silverware. In the back of the cabinet, she finds the faded Bugs Bunny glass that's been around for as long as she can remember. She also grabs the Speedy Gonzales glass, even though a mouse doesn't fit the day's theme.

While setting the table, Kennedy notices her mother's back-feather on a tile near the stove. Between two fingers she carries the feather to her place at the table, and sets what she hopes is a good luck charm on her phone.

"Everything all right, sweetie?" her mother says, studying her face.

"Yeah."

Kennedy devours her eggs and turkey bacon with abandon. She doesn't understand why the whole family has to eat fake bacon just because her dad has to, but at least she's somewhat used to the taste by now. While she's drinking her mango-orange juice, her brother comes in, gripping the Easter penguin by one ear. He positions the stuffed animal behind his plate and balances a spoon against the creature's pale pink stomach.

Kennedy thinks *Hello, Tomas, hello, Tomas* in his direction, but he doesn't turn to her or respond in any way. When he stabs at his bacon, the Easter penguin falls face-first onto a puddle of ketchup.

"Sorry," Tomas says, quickly removing the penguin from his plate.

"Don't worry about it," Kennedy says. "He looks like a vampire penguin now. I like it."

Tomas attempts to clean off the ketchup with his napkin and only makes the stain worse.

"Sorry," her brother says again.

At long last, Kennedy's phone vibrates with life. Alejandra writes, `dont play dum. you know why i'm mad.`

She punctuates the text with two frowny faces and yet another raging fox demon.

`I don't know why you're mad,` Kennedy writes back. `Just tell me.`

The teenager cracks her knuckles, one by one, and before she can finish, she gets another text back.

`you missed my bday party last night. you promised you would come!!!!!!!!`

`You never told me you were having a birthday party.`

`ahhhhhhh! what do you mean? just admit your mistake!`

`I'm really sorry.` Kennedy adds about a thousand penitent angels to the end of the text, but she knows that it won't be enough. How could she forget Alejandra's birthday? Try as she might, she can't recall a single mention of a party. On Friday, they talked about Steven Universe and what kind of YouTube star Alejandra should be and the plague.

"Who wants to take Uncle Marv his breakfast?" her mother says.

"I will," Kennedy says. She leaves her phone on the table, screen-down, and experiences a mild sensation of relief as she climbs the stairs. She does want to work things out with Alejandra, but at the same time, she wants to be as far from her phone as humanly possible.

She would probably join a mission to Mars right now, if given the opportunity.

Upstairs, she notices the plug-in air freshener on the floor. The white plastic is fractured. The metal prongs that go into the outlet are bent and twisted.

She finds Uncle Marv sitting in bed, his hands inside an old Amazon delivery box. From this angle, she can't see inside the box, but she's assuming this is part of his new project. A bottle of Elmer's glue lies on the pillow to his side.

"Oh, hi, Kennedy," he says, waving at her with a small drawing of a chair in his hand. "I'm a regular Tommy Wiseau, aren't I? Oh, hi."

"Who's Tommy Wiseau?" Kennedy says.

"Never mind."

Uncle Marv places the Amazon box in front of him, with the opening facing away from Kennedy. He must want the finished project to be a surprise.

Kennedy gives him a fork with the plate of breakfast, but he uses two fingers to lift the tiniest chunk of egg to his mouth. The morsel drops before he can even take a bite.

"What is that?" her uncle says, sniffing at the air. "Cinnamon bread?"

"Cinnamon buns. It's Sunday Bunday."

"Your family really likes cinnamon, huh?"

"It's Mom's favorite smell, remember?"

"Oh. Yeah."

Kennedy thinks it's strange that he would say "your family" when he's lived here since his divorce years and years ago. This is his home as much as hers.

Her uncle sits there, not eating, tapping his index finger against the side of his head. "So, what do you think about doing another one of our meditation sessions? I'd like a little more practice, if I'm going to teach my own class someday."

"Okay."

"Could you ask your mom and everyone? See who else wants to join in?"

"Yeah."

Downstairs, Kennedy forgets all about the meditation session because the cinnamon buns are out of the oven. The new why didn't you come? tell me the truth!!!!!!! text almost ruins her appetite, but she swallows the dessert anyway.

"We should get a real bunny for Bunday," Tomas says to her. "We could set him free on the haunted trail."

"It's not really haunted," Kennedy says. "Those paranormal investigators checked it out last October, remember? They couldn't find anything, except one guy said he felt someone touch his back. There weren't even any EVPs."

Tomas nods.

After she finishes her cinnamon bun, she heads for the stairs, but then she remembers what her uncle asked her. Her mom says yes to the meditation session, and her brother holds up the Easter penguin and says "Okay" in a gravelly voice. Kennedy doesn't ask her dad, because he doesn't like waking up early on Sundays, and because he doesn't like hippie-dippie crap. Her father calls it a worse word than *crap*, though.

In Uncle Marv's room, Kennedy takes her usual spot on the rug, on the golden phoenix with red eyes. He's holding a vine in his beak that spirals outward, blooming with angular flowers throughout the entire rug.

"Let's clear our minds," her mother sings, from the one chair in the room. "And have some good times. We'll be quiet as mimes. Do you like my rhymes?"

"No," Kennedy says.

From the bed, Uncle Marv taps at an empty Gatorade bottle with his finger. "Okay, I guess we better get started," he says. "So, um, you should all close your eyes and take a few deep breaths. Yeah, that's good. Now, when I say go, I want you to tighten all the muscles in your face for a second. Go." Uncle Marv works his way down the muscles in the body. The shoulders, the chest, the arms, on and on. They tighten the muscles and then let go. "Yeah, good. Now try to clear your mind. If your mind wanders somewhere, don't try to push that thought away. Observe the thought, like you're watching a TV screen, and eventually the thought will go away without a struggle. When you're trying to empty your mind, you don't want to struggle. Does that make any sense?" No one says anything, so he continues, "Okay, I'm going to stop talking now. Keep your eyes closed. Let everything go."

Kennedy's not one for sitting still, but she tries her best not to open her eyes or wriggle or toes. She pictures herself like a gargoyle on a gothic cathedral, dribbling rainwater through her pointed teeth. She listens to Uncle Marvin as he taps at the bottle. She listens to the rain peppering slantwise against the bedroom window. The sounds intensify and echo within her mind. Her body feels droopy and lifeless in a way that surprises her, even though she experiences this sensation every session.

While her body may not move, she imagines herself again as the gargoyle on the rooftop. A crack zigzags down her gray torso, and then the stone coating her body shatters into dust. Her eyes open, red and incandescent. She outstretches her wings, the golden feathers quivering as a groaning gale attempts to push her backward. Instead of stumbling back, she leaps into the wind, face-first, and she soars. Black clouds burst as she passes through them. Lightning strikes her body, but she feels nothing. From here, her mind wanders to a memory of her brother crying uncontrollably on a plane, throwing every toy they hand him onto the floor. "Shut up," her father says. "Can't you shut him up?" Uncle Marvin says, "Switch seats with me. Let me talk to him."

Her mind takes her away to another time and place, where she feels her foot pressing into wet cement. The plaster oozes between her toes. As she admires her print, Uncle Marv writes her name into the cement, using a chopstick.

She remembers walking around the artificial oak tree, holding Uncle Marvin's hand. "Somebody took the ugly pineapple man," Tomas yells. "No, he's right there," Uncle Marvin says, pointing.

In another memory, she's lying on her bed, buried under a mountain of stuffed penguins. Uncle Marvin adds a final emperor penguin in a tuxedo on the top. "Is that better?" Uncle Marvin says. "Yes," she lies. She loves being buried by penguins, but tonight, they can't help her. She feels itchy and slimy and sore. She wants the chicken pox germs inside her to die already. Uncle Marvin sits beside her and tells her a story about a duck whose bill falls off because he has the duck pox. The duck tries to replace his bill with a pinecone and a cattail and a pair of spoons that he finds inside the hollow of a tree. When he tries to talk to his badger friend, the spoons clank together and the badger dances around to the rhythm. The duck tries to dance too, but he ends up in a coughing fit. Eventually, he realizes that he needs to stop trying to pretend that he doesn't have the duck pox. He needs to take care of himself. He needs to rest.

After the story, Kennedy closes her eyes and wills herself not to scratch her skin. Uncle Marvin places a hand on her forehead, as if he's checking her temperature, but when she opens her eyes, veiny streaks of rosy red light travel down his arm. She can feel the light funneling into her head. Suddenly, she feels less itchy and slimy and sore. The here-and-now Kennedy, meditating in Uncle Marvin's room, isn't sure how anything like this could happen in real life. It was probably a fever dream. Then again, didn't she see that rosy red light another time, on the haunted trail, when Tomas cut his leg on a rock? Didn't Uncle Marvin glow a little then too?

She remembers a panting dog lacking the tip of his tongue, and the smell of her grandmother's candied yams, and that safe, warm feeling of her father carrying her to bed, and sparks of pale red light, and the clumpy red pieces of a dead rabbit in the haunted trail. The memories yank her from place to place, and she tries to observe the scenes like she's watching a TV screen. She tries not to push the thoughts away. Every other meditation session made her feel airy, like the golden phoenix. But now it's as if she's stuck on a roller coaster that won't stop looping. She remembers her mother weeping downstairs in the middle of the night, and a marble she accidentally swallowed pushing its way down her throat, and Uncle Marv's studio downtown with the papier-mâché T. rex and the zombified penguins and the art lessons. The memories press her from all sides. She tries to imagine the phoenix but his face contorts into the half-eaten head of the dead rabbit. The roller coaster feeling intensifies, and suddenly her head erupts with pain, and then she falls, fast and empty-headed into darkness.

When she opens her eyes, she can't recall why she's lying on the floor, looking up at a motionless ceiling fan. Then it comes back to her, in hazy bits and pieces. She remembers closing her eyes and thinking about the gargoyle and then there was darkness. She sits up and notices that her brother's gone. The only other person left in the room is Uncle Marv, who's working again on the Amazon box.

"I fell asleep," Kennedy says, stretching her arms to the ceiling.

"Yeah," Uncle Marv says, quietly, not meeting her eyes. "I thought I'd let you sleep, so you could recuperate a little bit."

Kennedy isn't sure why she would need to recuperate from meditation, but then again, Uncle Marv is the expert.

He sits on the bed, rubbing at both sides of his head with the tips of his index fingers.

"How's your box going?" Kennedy says.

"Oh, great," he says, glancing at her.

Pangs of curiosity detonate in her chest, because she wants to see inside the box, and she wants to see the red light in Uncle Marv's arms again. She wants to ask him how it feels when the energy dances up and down his skin. But she keeps her mouth shut. Uncle Marv has taught her, over and over, that the unraveling of a mystery can't be rushed. "You can't peek inside a chrysalis to see the butterfly early," he always says.

Looking at her phone, Kennedy realizes she has more pressing matters at hand than Uncle Marv's Amazon box or his spiritual energies. Not only does Alejandra wish Kennedy would drop dead, she doesn't want to be roommates when they go to college anymore. Kennedy doesn't want to die, exactly, but she doesn't want to be alive, either.

## Imani

Imani pricks her fingers with the embroidery needle four times in ten minutes, because she's rushing to finish the tiny clothes in time for the miracle. Marv tells her not to worry. He says the miracle will happen whether she finishes or not, but she worries anyway. She wants to do her part.

"*Sew* much fabric," she whispers. "*Sew* little time."

She knows that the grinning peanut statue would appreciate her pun, if he weren't in a thousand pieces. For a moment, she considers digging those shards out of the trash and gluing them back together, but she swiftly dismisses the thought. If Hendrick doesn't care about the death of the peanut man, then why should she?

After Imani takes a deep breath, she continues hand-sewing the felt tie to an ecru-colored dress shirt. She plays the podcast on her phone, but she only perceives fragments of their conversation. They mention an aunt who collects vintage mannequins in a barn. Later, they talk about a tea party attended by chemically treated corpses. The man who dug up the bodies shrouded their heads with layers and layers of Saran Wrap. He also kept laminated papers under their chairs, full of information like their blood type and their favorite foods. Normally, Imani would eat all this up, but her thoughts wander off again.

Sighing, she pauses her phone. The storm murmurs out the window, tapping at the glass. For a moment, she imagines a man standing on a ladder, peering into her bedroom, but she doesn't dignify the thought with any reaction whatsoever. She doesn't even turn to the window to check.

"Stop it," she says.

As she works, her thoughts gravitate back toward the miracle. Her palms sweat. Her hands tremble. According to Marv, no one will be in any danger during the miracle, but beyond that, she doesn't know what kind of phenomenon they can expect tonight. If she asks, he'll only tell her that to open a chrysalis early kills the butterfly. In time, her mind drifts back to the first time she experienced one of Marvin's marvels. She remembers that when her finger snapped, she left the apartment without saying another word. She walked toward Dairy Queen, her left arm pressed tight against her stomach. She tried to keep her hand perfectly still, but the broken pinky still sent shockwaves of agony up her arm. The wind stung her arms and her neck, because she forgot her jacket. She forgot everything.

Thankfully, an old woman in a purple hat gave her a quarter so that she could call Omar on the payphone. After the call, she continued on to the Dairy Queen, but she didn't have any money, so she sat out on a plaque in the yellowing grass. Omar said, "I'll be right there," but twenty minutes passed, and he didn't come.

She was about ready to walk to the emergency room herself when she spotted someone in her peripheral vision. She expected Omar, but she found a big-nosed guy in a puffy neon-orange jacket and a backward baseball cap.

Obviously, Imani can't recall their conversation word for word, but he started by saying something like, "Hey. I, uh, I know you don't know me from Adam, whoever the fuck Adam is. But I know you, sort of. I mean, I dream about you sometimes."

"I'm not interested," Imani said, standing up so that she could head into the Dairy Queen.

"I'm not hitting on you," the man said. "I'm sorry. I'm not explaining this very well." He rubbed at the middle of his forehead with an index finger. "I guess there's no explaining this in a way that would make sense to you. It barely makes any sense to me. But, um, I'm supposed to be here right now to help you."

"Did Omar send you?" she said.

"No. I was at home watching this movie called *The Baby* about this twentysomething-year-old guy who wears diapers and acts like a baby. Have you ever seen it?" Imani stared at him, and he continued. "Anyway, I was watching the movie, and I had this feeling I needed to be here by the Dairy Queen. I walked ten blocks. I didn't know exactly who or what I was supposed to find, but I found you. And like I said, I recognize you from some of my dreams."

By this time, Imani knew that she was speaking to someone with severe mental problems. He didn't come across as particularly dangerous, but she was frightened anyway.

The man sighed. "You're looking at me like I'm Belial Bradley. I mean, I get it. But, if you just look at my face a little bit, you'll see that you know me. The sort of dreams I've been experiencing aren't the one-sided kind. You've dreamed of me, too. If you look at me and you don't recognize me at all, I'll go away right now."

At that point, Imani made a show of staring at the man's face so she could say, "I don't know you." Then maybe he would leave her alone. But the problem was she did recognize him. Suddenly, she recalled seeing this man a dozen times, in castles and wastelands and clouds. She was always about to fall, and he reached out and caught her hand.

Imani opened her mouth to say, "Who are you?" but she found she couldn't speak.

"I'm Marvin," the man said, rubbing the back of his neck. "I wish we could sit and talk for a while before we get to this next part, but that never seems to be the nature of these meetings. What I'm saying is, there's no time for you to think this through. The energy's ready, and if we don't act now, we'll miss our chance." The man removed his jacket, and the teenager backed away a few steps. He held out his hand then. He closed his eyes. And wisps of coral fire hopped across his skin.

Imani wanted to run, of course, but she also couldn't keep her eyes off the roseate flames. She recognized this fire from her dreams as well.

"What do you want me to do?" she said, in a small voice that blew away in the icy wind.

With his eyes closed, Marvin said, "Not to rush you or anything, but I can't hold this forever. This is the time and the place. Even I can't change that."

Shivering in the cold, trembling in her fear, Imani stepped forward. She didn't understand any of this. But, somehow, she trusted this man from her dreams. She trusted the fire.

She reached out her left hand and Marvin said, "No, use your other one. I don't want to squeeze that pinky."

So, she gave him her good hand, and the fire spiraled around his arm and passed into her. Her heart pounded. Her body become warm, from top to bottom. She half expected her pinky to heal in the heat of that energy, but the pain never subsided. Instead, she visualized escaping her mother. This wasn't a new fantasy for her, of course, but this time, standing near the Dairy Queen, holding Marvin's hand, she didn't imagine herself as some hardened warrior. In the visualization, she was herself. She was a nail-biting, neurotic bundle of nerves. She didn't picture herself telling her mother off in some booming voice. She saw herself packing her bags, trembling. For years, she believed she needed to be stronger in order to escape her mother. But maybe that wasn't true. Maybe, despite her anxieties and her scars and her tears, she was strong enough already.

The fire on Marvin's arm disappeared, but the idea remained smoldering inside her.

"Well," he said. "That's all I can do for you right now, I guess. Unless you want a couple bucks for Dairy Queen?"

"No," she said. "Thank you."

He put on his jacket and made sure that his baseball cap was still pointing backward. "Well, I better go finish *The Baby*. It's good so far. Weird. You should check it out. Then we can talk about it the next time we meet. I'm not exactly sure when that'll be, but our destinies are definitely entwined." He interlaced his fingers, to emphasize the point. "Are you sure I can't buy you an ice cream?"

"No," she said. "I'm okay." And for the first time, in a very long time, she meant it.

## Tomas

In honor of Sunday Bunday, Tomas draws the stuffed

Easter penguin with bunny ears, only he gives the penguin three ears and one eye. He considers adding a few claws and fangs, but you're not supposed to start a game of Drawing Battle with too powerful of a fighter. In the end, he leaves the penguin rabbit largely vulnerable to most attacks.

He places the yellow notepad on Uncle Marv's bed and says, "Your turn."

"Hmm?" Uncle Marv touches the paper with his middle finger. "Oh, yeah. The battle thing. I'll get to this soon. But first, do you want to see a little sneak peek of the new project?" Using two fingers, he lifts a cardboard box from off the nightstand. "Only the background is done, but I thought maybe you'd want to see it first, since you contributed all the furniture and objects and everything."

Tomas nods, and Uncle Marv turns the box around so that the boy can see inside. What he sees is a diorama, like the one Tomas had to make for Mrs. Z about *Frog and Toad*. Tomas recognizes his potbelly stove and his dress form and his industrial sewing machine table.

"Give me a second," Uncle Marv says. "I'll show you something cool."

After a few moments, the drawings within the box become blurry and then bloat into three dimensions. A thread of black smoke snakes upward from the potbelly stove. Tomas touches the 3-D dress form, but it still only feels like paper. He smiles. He wants to shrink himself down so that he can play inside the box with the body-building mouse and the headless bobblehead and the army man who only fears balloons. In honor of Bunday, they could grill hamburgers on the potbelly stove.

Uncle Marv taps the top of the box. "After the miracle tonight, we'll be able to use this thing properly."

Tomas doesn't understand much about the miracles, except that years ago, he cut his leg on a rock and Uncle Marv healed him. Also, his uncle saved his dad's life once, but no one ever told him the details about that. Does the miracle tonight mean that someone else might die if Uncle Marv doesn't save them? The thought makes him feel sick to his stomach.

"Well, kid," his uncle says, opening a new bottle of Gatorade. "I need to rest up for tonight or I'm fucked. Sorry. Or I'm screwed."

When he moves the diorama from the bed to the nightstand, he knocks the yellow notebook onto the floor, next to a few empty bottles. Tomas reaches for the Drawing Battle pages, but he freezes in place when his uncle releases a high-pitched screech. Then he screams again.

"I'll get Mom," Tomas says, his voice quivering.

"No, don't worry, kid," Uncle Marv says, lying flat on his back now. "I know it sounded like I was yelling, but that wasn't me, exactly. The little barrier between me and the others broke down for a second, is all. That was them yelling through me. Anyway, you don't need to worry about any of this. I'm good. Really."

Hot tears fill the boy's eyes and he wipes at his face with both his hands. From here he can see into the cardboard box. Everything's flat and normal again.

"You'd better go," Uncle Marv says, his eyes closed. "I need to concentrate."

Tomas goes outside, leaving the yellow notebook on the floor, next to the trash. Inside his room, he closes his door and puts on his headphones and holds his breath. None of that helps. He hopes the miracle will happen soon, because maybe then he'll stop hearing his uncle's screams inside his head.

## Hendrick

Hendrick often wishes that someone would invent waterproof earbuds so that he could submerge himself completely in the tub while listening to Morgaine. If he breathed through a tube, then he wouldn't have to get out of the water during the entire session.

As it is, Hendrick has to sit up to keep the earbud wires from getting wet. He keeps his phone on a small table next to the tub, right next to his Old Fashioned. He only adds the maraschino cherry and the orange wheel during special occasions, and he can't think of anything more appropriate than a miracle night.

Through the earbuds, Morgaine tells Hendrick to close his eyes and take a few deep breaths. She has him tighten all the muscles in his face and then relax. Hendrick tightens his shoulders and chest and arms and hands. After he relaxes his toes, Morgaine tells him to clear his mind. If his mind wanders somewhere, she wants him to observe the thought like he's watching a TV screen.

Morgaine says that after she counts down from ten, Hendrick will be in her complete control. She'll be inside him then, and she'll be able to do anything she wants.

Once she finishes counting down, Hendrick doesn't feel any discernable change in his mind, but he does feel quite relaxed after all that deep breathing and tensing and relaxing. Morgaine commands him to watch her while she removes her velvet dress and her black lingerie. As she strips for him, Hendrick can sometimes see her dark emerald eyes, her eager breasts, the slit of tongue he can glimpse between her barely open lips. He never sees her in her entirety during these sessions, but he doesn't mind. Morgaine commands him to sit still while she massages her tits. She says, by the end of this, she'll make him come without him ever touching himself. During the past four months or so, she's never managed to accomplish this, but Hendrick doesn't mind that, either.

As always, Hendrick imagines himself inside Brett's apartment. Sometimes, she kneels while he sits on the leather couch. Sometimes, the two of them climb onto the pool table. Hendrick pictures himself in a real place so that the universe knows he would welcome this as a reality. Obviously, Hendrick doesn't have the same kind of powers as Marvin, but these visualizations are supposed to help manifest his desires in some way. Hendrick doesn't quite understand the process, and he doesn't care to, really.

After the audio ends, Hendrick finishes and dries himself off. In the bedroom, Imani's still hard at work on those weird little doll clothes Marvin asked her to create. She seems so excited about tonight, and for a moment, Hendrick feels a little guilty. Even after all these years, his wife doesn't understand that the miracles exist to benefit Marvin and Hendrick alone. Sure, Marvin has healed children on numerous occasions, but only because Hendrick didn't want them to suffer. Years ago, when Hendrick desired a wife, Marvin found Imani and brought the two of them together. Hendrick remembers that morning when Marvin dragged him to that thrift shop with the giant hamburger man. Imani rushed over to

Marvin and said, "It's you." And Marvin said, "Yeah. Hey. This is my brother Hendrick."

Imani still believes, in her naive way, that Marvin's powers are good and pure. Sometimes, Hendrick wants to tell her the truth, but he knows he never will.

Lying on the bed in his damp T-shirt and boxers, Hendrick wonders what's coming tonight. He would ask Marvin, but his brother would only give him that stupid spiel about the chrysalis and the butterfly. The truth is probably that Marvin doesn't know exactly what he's going to accomplish with that light of his until it's actually happening.

Of course, Hendrick hopes that tonight's event will somehow bring Morgaine into his life or at least a Ferrari 599 GTB Fiorano. When all's said and done, though, he trusts in his brother's creepy powers, and he'll take what he can get.

## Kennedy

Alejandra no longer wants Kennedy to drop dead, but she still doesn't think the two of them should be roommates in five years. Alejandra wants to live alone now, in a studio apartment with a loft bed. Aly ends her final text with only one daisy emoji, even though she usually says goodnight with at least five.

Every sleeping position Kennedy attempts feels worse than the last, so she sits up and grabs her book. She reads the same paragraph over and over again for about a thousand hours.

After tossing the book across the room at her backpack, she heads for the bathroom and pauses in front of Uncle Marv's door. He said this specific miracle required silence and concentration, so he didn't want to be disturbed tonight. Kennedy doesn't see how pressing her ear against the door could disturb him any, so she decides to go ahead.

At first, she can only hear the perpetual chatter of the rainstorm. Then Uncle Marv shouts, in a muffled voice, "Hey, Kennedy. Come in."

Kennedy hesitates for a moment, but then she opens the door and steps inside. When it comes to her uncle's miracles, she knows she should expect the unexpected. And yet she still experiences a jolt of shock when she finds him lying stomach-down on the rug, rosy flames rising from his back. The light of the fire blinds her a little, and she squints her eyes.

"Hey," Uncle Marv says, his head turned to the side, facing her. "I know I said I wanted to be alone and all, but I'm really up shit's creek in here. Sorry. Crap's creek. Could you scratch my back for a while? That's all I need, really. I'd do it myself, but I can barely move my arms. This whole miracle thing took a lot out of me this time around."

Kennedy takes a step forward. "What about the fire?"

"Oh, that? It won't hurt you. You won't even feel it."

Slowly, Kennedy brings a finger close to one of the undulating flames. Like Uncle Marv said, she doesn't feel any heat whatsoever.

Uncle Marv clears some phlegm from his throat and says, "If you could hurry, that would be great. I think I might be dying here."

Kennedy wants to hurry, but her body won't cooperate. In slow motion, she plunges her trembling hands into the flames. The brightness of the fire hurts her eyes, so she turns her head to the side. She runs her fingers across his back as if she's casually rubbing at an itch. His skin feels slimy and smooth.

"Use your nails," her uncle says, his voice cracking.

"I bit off all my nails," Kennedy says.

"Well, do the best you can."

Kennedy presses a little harder, and his skin bends to her touch. She feels as if she's digging her fingers into a slightly deflated, wet balloon.

"Keep going," he says. "I think we're almost there."

Kennedy continues scratching away, more vigorously than before, and finally his back bursts. The popping sound startles her into jumping backward. She wants to ask her uncle if he's all right, but her voice refuses to come out. Before she can speak, her uncle's mystical flames fade away, revealing the pallid, mangled skin of his back.

"Oh, shit," Uncle Marv says, weakly. "Oh, shit."

When she glances at her uncle's face, she can see only a smear of color where his face should be.

"Oh, shit," he says again.

"I'll get my mom," Kennedy says.

"No, wait. Don't open the door. We need to keep them contained in here. You'd better lock the door so that no one opens it from the outside."

Kennedy doesn't understand what any of that means, but she locks the door anyway. Ruining a miracle is the last thing in the world she wants to do. The teenager takes a deep breath and turns back around. Uncle Marv's still lying on the rug, his face turned away from her now. After a few moments, the tattered flesh of his back quivers. Kennedy hopes that his skin is in the process of re-forming itself and healing, but that doesn't seem to be the case at all, because a small creature wriggles out of the carnage. Only, he's not a creature at all, is he? He looks like a tiny, bald version of Uncle Marv. He crawls on all fours in her direction, opening and closing his mouth silently, coated with translucent slime. Kennedy backs away until her back is pressed against the door.

At this point, another tiny uncle squirms his way out of Uncle Marvin's shredded skin, and then another. The first Lilliputian slides off of Uncle Marvin and then makes a run for it. He stumbles a few times but swiftly makes his way under the bed.

"I know this is a lot to ask," Uncle Marv says. "But could you help me catch these guys? I need them all in one place, as close together as possible. Put them in a drawer, I guess."

Kennedy simultaneously wants to escape into the hallway and hold one of the tiny people in her hands to verify if they're real. In the end, she takes a deep breath and creeps forward. She grabs at one of the little guys who just tumbled onto the rug, but he slips from her fingers like a wet bar of soap. She thinks of the net she and Tomas use to catch frogs on the haunted trail, but that's in Tomas's closet. After surveying the room, she grabs a pillow from off the bed and removes the pillowcase. She easily slips the case over a Marvin who's still attempting to wrestle himself free from the tangle of back skin. Then, trapped in the fabric, he releases a high-pitched shriek. The other tiny Marvins in the room join him in a discordant chorus. After a few seconds, they pause for breath at the same time, and then they scream again.

"Goddammit, you guys," Uncle Marv says. He attempts to push himself up off the floor, but his elbows buckle and he collapses to the rug. On the second try, he manages to sit up. His face still looks hazy, like before, but she can tell that he's frowning.

"I'll get them," Kennedy says, dumping the trapped Marvin into a drawer. Thanks to all the screaming, she has an easy time finding the little Marvins in all their hiding places. When she reaches for one of them, he dashes between her legs and attempts to scale the curtains. She traps him right after he falls onto his back.

Kennedy jumps when someone knocks at the door.

"Marv!" her mother says, and pounds at the door again. "Open the door!"

Uncle Marv rubs his forehead for a while, and then the knocking stops. Her mother doesn't say another word out there.

"Don't worry," her uncle says. "We'll explain everything to her after we're done in here. For now, we need to get all of them together before I pass out. And we really don't want them to stay like this for very long. They might get hungry."

Kennedy nods, even though she doesn't understand in the least. One at a time, she collects the Marvins and empties them into the drawer. They still won't stop screeching.

"Okay, I think that's all of them," her uncle says, finally.

He's still sitting on the rug, barely moving, his face little more than a pale smudge above his neck. "Could you bag them all up and bring them over to me? I don't think I can walk yet."

In order to transfer the little men into the pillowcase, she has to pull open the drawer, pluck one out, and close the drawer again quickly before the others can climb over the edge. The Marvins kick and squirm in her hand, but she manages not to lose any.

Once she hands over the writhing sack to her uncle, he says, "Thanks, kid. You really saved my butt." Then he holds the pillowcase right in front of his face. Kennedy half expects some fire to erupt from his eyes, but he only sits there, frozen.

After a few seconds, the tiny people stop screaming, and Uncle Marv slumps over on his side. Only, he's not Uncle Marv anymore. He's something white and gray, like the moon, with a lipless slit for a mouth.

When he opens his eyes, he says, "Oh, shit." A moment later, his face glimmers and then he looks like his regular self again. "That wasn't . . . I didn't mean to scare you like that. I'm sorry."

"I wasn't scared," Kennedy says. Of course, she's lying, and her hands are shaking, but she doesn't want her uncle to feel bad. "Why did you look like that? Was it part of the miracle?"

"Yeah," he says, looking down at his hands. "Just an aspect of my soul manifesting itself. It's hard to explain."

"You looked really cool."

Marvin meets her eyes for a moment and laughs a little through his nose. "Well, I'd better rest before my brain implodes." He swings the limp pillowcase back and forth in front of him. "Before you go, could you dump these guys back in the drawer?"

"Yeah." Instead of pouring the small Marvins out of the sack, she slowly boosts them out one at a time. Their limbs droop at strange angles, as if they're all double-jointed. She lines them up carefully on a folded pair of sweatpants. She stares at them for a while, and she can see their small chests rising and falling as they sleep. Suddenly, a twenty-foot wave of drowsiness hits her. She yawns.

When she turns to Uncle Marv to say goodnight, she finds him curled up on the rug with his eyes closed, and his Klingon T-shirt back on.

"Do you want me to help you up on the bed?" she says.

"Nah," he says. "I'm good."

While she bends back the fingers of her left hand, she considers asking him one more time if he needs help getting into the bed. In the end, though, she leaves without another word, and closes the door behind.

In her own bed, she can feel the darkness of sleep closing in on her almost immediately. During those final moments of consciousness, she replays the miracle a few times in her head. At the appointed time, the tiny Marvins materialized on the rug, in a burst of pale pink fire. They stood, side by side by side, all eight of them. They smiled at her and waved before nodding off to sleep. And Marvin told Kennedy to rest up as well, because tomorrow was a big day. Tomorrow was the beginning of her new life.

# MONDAY

## *Imani*

Imani sets her weekday alarm for 6:00 A.M., but Marv wakes her up at an even ungodlier hour, saying, "Hey, guys. Guys. I have something to give you."

Hendrick rolls to his other side and says, "Shut the fuck up, Marv."

"Okay, well, I'll give your miracle to someone else, then."

With that, her husband groans and sits up, his eyes barely open.

So, at four thirty in the fucking morning, Marv leads the whole family downstairs for their cryptic gifts, like a parent escorting his children to the tree on Christmas morning. In the living room, Marvin turns to them, smiling a little. He rubs at the area between his eyes with a pinky. "So, uh, I know what you're going to think about all this, and I get it. All I ask is that you give these guys a chance. They exist to help you and to keep you safe and to transform your lives in substantial ways. Just, you know, keep that in mind."

Imani has no clue what her brother-in-law's talking about, but she follows him into the kitchen. The instant she spots the so-called miracles, her whole body tenses. Sitting cross-legged on the dinner table, two of the small Marvs wave and three of them say "Hey" simultaneously. They're wearing the little clothes Imani finished up the night before.

"What the fuck is this?" Hendrick says.

Marv walks over and picks one of the tiny men up. "Like I said, they're here to help us. They're manifestations of spiritual energies and arcane truths. It's hard to explain." Marv goes on rambling, talking about the family's potential for transformative growth, but Imani turns her attention to her son. He's sniffling now, at her side. She takes his hand and leads him into the living room. He continues sniffling, staring at his bare feet. He doesn't let go of her hand.

"You don't have to look at them," Imani says. "I'll make Uncle Marv send them away. I'm going to get your sister and then I'll be right back."

He nods.

Back in the kitchen, Imani says to Kennedy, "Put that thing down and go to your room. Take your brother with you. Tell him I'll be right there."

"I don't want to go," her daughter says, holding the

monstrosity close to her face.

"Kennedy, now."

Her daughter sighs, and carefully sets the thing on her penguin parade place mat. A moment later, the miniature man vomits clear liquid. "Sorry," the creature says, in a small, cartoonish voice.

"They get a little motion-sick," Marv says. "Once we get some ginger into them, they should be all right."

After Kennedy stalks off, Imani says, "Honey, I need you upstairs."

Hendrick grunts a little in response, and Marv says, "Take all the time you need to talk this over. It's a big step, I know." He grins a little, and the small Marvins on the table smile with him.

Imani finds her children in Kennedy's room, watching some meowing cat video on the girl's phone. Tomas snorts with laughter.

"Are you guys all right?" Imani says.

Without looking up at her, they both say, "Yeah."

"Okay. I'll be right back. I need to talk with your dad."

Imani rushes through the hall and finds her husband lying on top of the covers with his eyes closed.

"Hendrick," she says.

"Huh?" He sits up and rubs his face.

"I don't want those things in my house."

"They're not things," Hendrick says, scratching at the

underside of his nose. "They're beings of spiritual energy or whatever Marv said."

"I don't give a fuck what they are." Imani straightens one of the picture frames on the wall. "They scare Tomas, and they scare me, too. You're really going to sit there and tell me they don't freak you the fuck out?"

Hendrick shrugs. "They look like Marv. And they're four inches tall. They're not exactly intimidating."

Imani sighs. Whenever they're dealing with a Marv situation, Hendrick always takes his side. "Hendrick. Do you really want these things around our kids?"

"Marv says the little guys can keep Kennedy and Tomas safe. These are divine beings, Im. They're like angels."

"They are not fucking angels." Imani moves over to the bookshelf and she decides that she wants to transfer the red books to the top shelf. When she was a kid, she used to organize her books and magazines by color.

She can hear the creaking of the floor as Hendrick climbs off the bed and approaches her. "I know they're weird," he says. "But when have Marv's miracles ever hurt us in any way? When has Marv ever steered us wrong with his advice or his spiritual insights?" He stands beside her now, yawning. "These manifestations or whatever they are, Marv says they can help us in ways we can't even imagine. But you don't even want to try, because you don't trust anybody. Not even Marv, who healed our kids and saved my life and brought the two of us together. You think we're all your mom out to get you."

"This isn't about that," Imani says, searching for another red spine. "When I look at those little monsters, I—" Before she can finish her thought, her legs buckle with pain and the hardwood floor slams against her face. Darkness closes in at the edge of her vision, like storm clouds rolling swiftly across a bright blue sky. For a moment, she can see Marv's white sneakers in the doorway.

The shadows that overtake her re-form into a flurry of leaves that brush against her consciousness. She recognizes the ancient oaks and the arroyo willow trees and the bracken ferns. She spots a pair of red-winged blackbirds glaring at one another on top of two broad-leaved cattails. An enormous catfish thrusts its head out of the quiet pond, hoping for a piece of bread meant for the ducks. No one's supposed to feed the ducks here, but people do anyway. She can see Tomas crumpled on the dirt, gushing too much blood from his leg. "Marvin," Imani says. "Do something. Please." Marv kneels then and rubs at his temples with his index fingers. A fire ignites in front of him, the color of pale pink manzanita flowers. Eight small men walk out of the flames and place their hands on Tomas's leg, and the wound begins to close. When they're finished, they wave at her and return to the fire again. "Thank you," Imani says, and she hopes they can hear her, wherever they are.

Then she's standing on half-dead grass in front of the Dairy Queen. The man in the puffy neon-orange jacket says, "If you just look at my face a little bit, you'll see that you know me. The sort of dreams I've been experiencing aren't the one-sided kind. You've dreamed of me, too, and my helpers. If you look at me and you don't recognize me at all, I'll go away right now."

Imani stares at his face so that he'll leave her the hell alone, but she does recognize him after all. She's seen him hundreds of times, in castles and wastelands and magical forests. When she's about to fall, he reaches out to catch her hand. When she's tied up, the little helpers appear and bite through the rope. When she's feeling like shit, the small men sing together in chorus and make her smile.

Now she's back on the haunted trail, and Marv points a pinky at the bobcat skulking a few yards away. "Don't worry," Marv says. "He won't hurt us." And as she watches the small creature staring into a ground squirrel hole, her body relaxes a little. She opens her mouth to speak, but the vibrant colors of the chaparral rush past her and she's in Marv's room again. Her brother-in-law says, "They're celestial beings, like angels." And at the dinner table, he says, "I can't summon them for very long yet, but one day I'll be strong enough to bring them here permanently." And next to the hamburger-headed man with the spatula and the butcher knife, Hendrick says, "The helpers saved my life once, back in San Diego." "What happened?" she says, but her voice sounds very far way. The thrift shop swirls around her, forming streaks of light across her vision. People speak to her from every direction. At first, she can discern a few individual words. Divine. Steadfast. Safe. The cacophony of voices intensifies until the sounds bleed together into a steady, incomprehensible murmuring. She wants to cover her ears, but she doesn't seem to have any hands.

When Imani opens her eyes again, she's lying on the floor in her bedroom, next to the bookcase. She stands and finds her husband asleep on the bed. She feels a nebulous urge to wake him up, but the alarm hasn't even gone off yet.

She finds her children awake already in Kennedy's room, watching videos on the girl's phone. They look up at her, with eager looks on their faces.

"Uncle Marv is ready for us now," Imani says.

It feels like Christmas morning as she leads the two of them downstairs. She can tell they're excited, because neither of them say a word all the way to the dining table.

Marv's waiting for them, with the little helpers sitting cross-legged on their place mats.

"Remember what Uncle Marv said," Imani says. "They're celestial beings, but they're not invincible on this plane of existence. You have to be careful with them."

"We know, Mom," Kennedy says.

As her children pick up their helpers, Imani feels a few pangs of fear, but that's only natural. Marv told her she would feel somewhat apprehensive in the presence of the helpers, in the beginning. But beyond her worries lies a profound sense of relief. Almost every day, she feels like a con artist in this house, pretending that she knows what she's doing, pulling off only two-bit impersonations of mothers she's seen on TV. Maybe now, with celestial beings involved, she won't accidentally ruin her children. Maybe now she can finally relax.

## Tomas

As always, Pablo spends the majority of lunch telling Tomas about the UFO in his garage. Pablo says the machine can now hover two inches off the ground. Months ago, when the boy first started talking about the invention, Tomas believed his friend, at least a little. But then, when Tomas went over to Pablo's house, his friend said, "We can't go into the garage now because of the radiation. We have to keep everything locked up." And then, when Pablo was in the bathroom, Tomas peeked into the garage and only saw two black cars and some fishing equipment.

Now, at the lunch table, Pablo says, "I think I'll be done in a few more months."

"That's cool," Tomas says.

"When I'm done, I'll probably paint a skull on it, or a dragon head."

At the bottom of his paper lunch bag Tomas finds a neon-orange sticky note that says, *You are the bee's knees. You are the crow's toes. You are the boulder's shoulders.* In his mind, he can hear his mother's voice speaking the words. He feels a little bad about throwing away his mom's note with the paper bag, but he doesn't need to keep the actual paper. He can think back on any school day and see her words written there in the memory.

After exiting the cafeteria to the playground, Tomas and Pablo sit on the cement ring surrounding their usual tree. They take out their notebooks and decide to see who can draw the most disgusting zombified dinosaur.

Tomas tries to keep his attention focused on the page when Everest walks over and flicks his shoulder.

"Spot," Everest says. "Hey, Spot." He flicks Tomas's shoulder again, even harder than before. "Mark thinks you're a mutant because your mom drank poison before you were born. She was probably drinking it so she could kill you. She's probably really mad that you're not dead."

"Shut up," Pablo says.

"You want me to flick you, too, Pablo?"

"No."

Everest wanders off then, because he never stays anywhere for very long. Even in the classroom, he always asks if he can be excused to use the bathroom.

After biting at his pencil for a while, Pablo says, "Wanna play handball?"

"No," Tomas says.

"Okay."

Pablo rushes off to the handball court and leaves his open notebook behind, without even finishing his dinosaur's rotting head.

Tomas likes handball well enough, but he doesn't want anyone to hear him sniffling. He doesn't want anyone to see his face, in case a tear manages to get out.

"That Everest is a real piece of shit," the helper says, in a small high-pitched voice. "Sorry. A piece of crap."

The boy unzips the front pocket of his Gigan backpack so that he can see inside. Tomas wishes he could take the poor helper out, because he looks uncomfortable curled up in there with his russet-brown tunic all bunched up and twisted.

"I thought we weren't supposed to talk here," Tomas whispers.

"Yeah, that's not a hard-and-fast rule or anything. More of a suggestion. As long as we're not calling too much attention to ourselves, we'll be fine." He stretches his arms above his head. "So, that Everest kid, does he do stuff like this often?"

Tomas shrugs and sniffles again. He wipes at his right eye before the helper can see the tear.

"Well, you don't have to tell me," the helper says. "I already know he's been flicking you all year. I can see it. And the shit he says to you. Jeez." Little Uncle Marv massages his tiny chin with his index finger and thumb. "The problem is, this kid will keep picking on you forever unless his soul reaches a state of enlightenment. Now, Big Marv can help us with this, but first we need to get Everest to your house."

Tomas doesn't understand what *enlightenment* means, but the thought of inviting Everest to his home makes another tear come out.

The helper sighs. "Look, I get where you're coming from, kid. But you can't deal with all your problems by drawing or crying or looking at your shoes. We need to make this playground a no-drama zone, where we can face your fears head on. That's what your dad always tells you to do, isn't it? Can you do that with me?"

"I don't know," Tomas says. "I want to play handball."

"Well, if you ever decide that you don't want to be a

scared little boy anymore, let me know. I can help you get stronger. I can protect you. Trust me."

Tomas zips up his backpack and walks toward the handball court. On his way there, he spots Everest sitting with Mark near the soccer field, yanking out blades of grass. Tomas holds his breath. He's not exactly sure how a tiny man in his backpack could protect him, but Little Uncle Marv probably has some special powers. The helpers did heal Tomas after he cut his leg, after all. They saved his dad's life in San Diego.

Staring at Everest now, Tomas does feel a little safer. A little stronger. Maybe one day he will invite Everest over to his house to play, only they won't play at all, and then Uncle Marv will take care of everything.

## Hendrick

Hendrick leaves work early for another doctor's appointment, but of course he hasn't visited Dr. Moon since his checkup last year, and he's not planning on seeing the man again any month soon. Instead, Hendrick drives toward the mall where a nine-year-old girl was shot in the chest last year. Imani won't take the kids there anymore.

Steering his crappy old Corolla with one hand, Hendrick connects his phone to the FM transmitter, and then he listens to Morgaine's voice through the car stereo. In her raspy voice, she tells him that she's in complete control. She commands him to sit perfectly still while she slips her middle finger into her mouth. Sometimes, while he's stopped at a light or cruising on an empty street, he closes his eyes for a few seconds. Sometimes, when he's in a busier area, he glances at the people on the street, searching for Morgaine's dark emerald eyes or her long, wavy hair that always drapes down over her breasts.

To be honest, Hendrick feels somewhat awkward, listening to Morgaine with the tiny man tucked away inside his leather messenger bag. But then again, Marv said this thing isn't a human being in any sense. It only exists to help Hendrick achieve his goals.

Hendrick roves around in the mall, squandering his hundred-dollar bills on a poplin shirt with mother-of-pearl buttons, a neon sign that says LIVE SHOW, and a bag of cinnamon pretzel chunks. When he first started shopping in this mall, he would hem and haw and search each store thoroughly before making a decision. He kept thinking about how one day his stash would run out. Now, when Hendrick enters a store, he darts in a random direction and grabs whatever happens to catch his fancy. He had to train himself to shop in this manner, and he's glad that he did.

While wandering, Hendrick continues to keep an eye

out for anyone who looks like Morgaine. The closest he comes to finding her is an eyeless mannequin draped in black velvet, with barely open lips. He considers asking the manager of the goth store if he could purchase her, but he's positive such a request would come to nothing. Stepping out of the goth store, Hendrick sighs. He's carried the messenger bag (and the small Marv) with him at all times, but the little creature's juju hasn't accomplished anything whatsoever. Perhaps his creature is defective in some way?

On his way out of the mall, Hendrick spots a Mr. Peanut bobblehead in one of the display windows. He hesitates for a moment, because this outing isn't supposed to be about Imani. But in the end, he buys the toy to replace the ugly peanut figurine his wife broke the other night. That should score him a few points, at least.

When he reaches the apartment complex, he leaves Mr. Peanut in the trunk and carries the rest of his haul up to Brett's place. First things first, he fills his Waldorf Hotel whiskey glass with some forty-year-old liquor. He doesn't sit down quite yet, because there are water bottles and granola-bar wrappers all over the carpet. With his glass in hand, Hendrick kicks all the trash back into Brett's territory. Hendrick considers leaving a note, but then again, Brett's doing him a favor, letting him rent a quarter of this place.

"Hey, can you let me out now?" the creature says from inside the messenger bag.

"Yeah, sure." Hendrick reaches in the bag and tosses the creature onto the couch. The little monstrosity vomits a moment later, and Hendrick rushes to the kitchenette for some paper towels.

"That couch is only six months old," Hendrick says.

"Sorry," the creature says, backing away from the vomit stain. "Can I have a bit of that towel? I got a little on myself."

While Hendrick cleans up the couch, the creature wipes at his pastel pink jacket and red pants. The man feels mildly repulsed every time he glances at the monster, mostly due to the grotesque outfit he's wearing.

"So," the monster says. "I can help you get this Morgaine woman, but I can't conjure her out of thin air. That's impossible, even for me."

Hendrick feels somewhat surprised that the creature knows so much about his thoughts, but that's spiritual beings for you, he supposes.

Before he has a chance to respond, the creature continues. "What I can do is change a woman so that she looks like Morgaine to you. I could even change Imani, but I'm guessing that's not the scenario you're looking for. Am I right?"

"Yeah."

The little creature taps at his forehead, just like the real Marv. "So, you need another woman. You could try a bar or one of those dating apps, I guess. Or, if you want to get this going right now, you could use that purple notebook Brett told you about. It's up to you, Hen."

"Don't call me Hen." After gulping down a few mouthfuls of whiskey, Hendrick strolls into the kitchenette and plucks the Lakers notebook from the top of the fridge. He finds the page with names like Cupcake and Kandi and Ambyr written in red ink. Next to each name is a price, a star rating, and other relevant information. All he would have to do is call up one of these women, using Brett's house phone, and he could have Morgaine within the next hour. He would have to be careful, of course. He'd need to use one of the condoms in Brett's bucket, and he'd need to shower before going home. He'd need to check himself in the mirror and make sure that his experience with Morgaine wasn't showing at all on his face.

Hendrick chooses one of the women with five stars and heads over to Brett's '60s-style rotary phone. He picks up the handset. He feels a little nauseous.

"This might not be the best idea," Hendrick says. "Who knows what kind of STDs I could pick up from these kinds of women. I should probably try out a bar instead."

By now, the creature's climbed to the top of the leather

couch. He says, "I know you inside and out, bro, and you're only—" The creature slips and falls behind the couch, screaming as he flails his arms. "Oh, fuck. Fuck, that hurt. I'm fine, by the way. Thanks for your concern." The monster rubs the back of his head. "As I was saying, I know you. I mean, I'm not Marv exactly, but I might as well be. And you're not hesitating right now because of venereal diseases. You need to be honest with yourself and accept the fact that this is difficult for you. You might not be in love with Imani the way that you used to, but she still has her tendrils inside you. Right?"

Hendrick returns the handset to the cradle and heads back to the couch for his whiskey.

"Well, you don't have to say anything," the monster says, clambering up the couch. "I know your mind. And I can help make all this so much easier for you, but I'm going to need some information from you first."

And so, for the next hour, Hendrick searches his mind for the details the imp requires. He feels sick to his stomach most of the hour, and more than once he thinks, *Buddy, you're a fool.* He probably shouldn't open himself up to a monster like this. When all's said and done, though, Hendrick doesn't mind being a fool if it means he can finally live the life he's always deserved.

## *Kennedy*

On the way to school, Kennedy collected a bundle of daisies next to the upside-down VW full of bees. The overgrown field scraped at her ankles and made her eyes puff up a little, but she didn't care. During fourth period, she gave Alejandra the flowers, along with her dancing-doughnut backpack charm. Alejandra said, "Thank you," but that was all.

Now that school's over, the two of them walk together as usual. The problem is that Alejandra stays a few steps ahead of her, and whenever Kennedy tries to catch up, her friend quickens her pace even more.

"Alejandra, please," the girl says.

But her friend won't slow down, and she won't respond.

After Alejandra turns right at the dentist's office, Kennedy continues forward alone.

"Hey, sorry about your friend," Fantastico says from inside her backpack.

"I thought we weren't supposed to talk in public."

"Well, yeah, but this isn't super public. Why don't you take out your phone, and then anyone who sees you will think you're talking on speaker."

Kennedy holds her phone out in front of her a little. Despite the agony of Alejandra's silent treatment,

Kennedy feels energized at the thought of asking Fantastico all the questions she formed throughout the day. "You really don't mind me calling you Fantastico? I can change it to Marv, if that's better."

"Nah," the helper says from behind her back. "I'm connected with your uncle, but I have my own consciousness, in a sense. I don't mind being called something different. Fantastico's good."

Kennedy hops over a crack in the cement that looks a little like a half-closed eye. "So, what are you, exactly?"

Fantastico's silent for a few seconds. "I'm a . . . a manifestation of spiritual energies and arcane truths."

"Yeah, Uncle Marv said that. But what does it mean, exactly?"

"It's hard to explain. I guess you could say I'm a set of goals brought to life in the physical realm. I exist to achieve those goals. Does that make any sense? Anyway, the point is, I can help you with whatever it is you need help with."

"Thanks for doing that."

"Yeah. No problem."

Kennedy hops up on top of a retaining wall in front of the gothic-style cathedral with all the spires and elongated windows. The farther she walks on the wall, the higher she rises from the sidewalk. For a moment, she imagines the retaining wall fracturing and spouting pale, bloated corpses. She pushes the thought from her mind and considers what she might want from a supernatural being like Fantastico. She needs a little help with her algebra homework, but her mom usually covers that. Could Fantastico give her some advice on how to deal with Alejandra?

Kennedy gets to the point on the wall where it's too high to jump, so she has to retrace her steps a little and leap off from there.

"Hey," Fantastico says. "Why don't you tell Alejandra you were sick during the weekend. You could say you were too sick to go to her party."

Kennedy spits out the top button of her flannel shirt that she's been gnawing on. "She wouldn't believe that, because I didn't ever mention that before. And anyways, I don't want to lie to her."

"Okay, well. Maybe you could make her one of those mix CDs, like you did last year."

"How do you know about that?" Kennedy pushes the crosswalk button four times, because that's one of her luckiest numbers.

"I know everything your uncle knows."

"But Uncle Marv never knew about that mix CD. Can you read my mind or something?"

"Well, sometimes I need to delve a little into your past experiences so that I can figure out how best to help you.

I haven't seen every moment of your life or anything, but I can usually find what I need to find."

Before Kennedy can formulate any follow-up questions, a man in a dark blue tracksuit stops right in front of her and says, "Hi."

Kennedy stops too and spits her top button out of her mouth.

"Do you live around here," the man says, scratching the side of his face. The way he says it, his sentence doesn't sound at all like a question.

"I have to go," Kennedy says.

"Why? What's wrong? I haven't done anything, have I?"

"I have to go," she says again, and when she tries to walk past the man, he steps to his side and blocks her.

"Why are you—" The tracksuit man doubles over and clutches at his stomach. "What the fuck!" he says. "What the fuck! What the fuck!"

Kennedy easily sidesteps the man now, and she surges faster than usual toward her street.

"Did you do that?" Kennedy says.

"Well, yeah," the high-pitched voice says behind her.

"What did you do to him?"

"I, uh. It's a little hard to explain, but I made him think he was recently stabbed in the stomach by a duck. The duck had knives for bills, and when the duck tried to talk, the tracksuit guy's insides all spilled out. It's all I could come up with on the spur of the moment."

"Wow," Kennedy says. "Cool."

When she gets home, the first thing the girl does is take Fantastico out of her bag and give him a gentle hug with one hand.

"Thanks for what you did," she says.

Fantastico taps his chin with finger, over and over. "It was nothing."

After setting her helper down next to the Easter Island head, she dumps the contents of her backpack onto her desk. She likes to finish all her homework as early as possible so she can enjoy the rest of the night without freaking out and biting off all her nails.

"Do you know anything about algebra?" the teenager says.

"Well, I'm not much of a math guy," Fantastico says, leaning against the stone head on her desk.

Instead of grabbing her textbook, Kennedy picks up today's sticky note from her mom. It says, *You are the bee's knees. You are the deer's ears. You are the crane's brains.* Her mom's messages never make much sense, but she doesn't really mind. She tosses the sticky note inside the drawer with all the other crinkled Post-its.

Before she loses her motivation for homework, Kennedy opens up her purple binder. As for her helper, he sits cross-legged on a marble coaster. When he unbuttons his leather jacket, he reveals a T-shirt underneath.

Kennedy points a mechanical pencil in his direction. "What's with the flaming skull thing on your shirt? Is that some sort of like celestial symbol?"

"Nah," Fantastico says, running his palm down the face of the skull. "This outfit's inspired by that greaser guy from *The Garbage Pail Kids Movie.* Your dad's Marvin is wearing an approximation of Howard the Duck's outfit in that scene where he plays the electric guitar. There's no real rhyme or reason to any of our outfits, I guess. Your Uncle Marv thought it would be fun."

"I think you look really cool."

"Thanks."

Fantastico lies back on the coaster and stares up at the ceiling. After a while, he holds his hands out in front of his face and looks at them. Kennedy wonders what a set of goals manifested into the physical realm thinks about when he daydreams.

Looking down at her notebook, Kennedy dreads the hours of busywork ahead of her, and all four of her limbs ache with the thought that Alejandra might not text her back all evening. But later tonight, maybe she'll have time to ask Fantastico some more questions and possibly unlock some mysteries of the universe. At least then her Monday won't be a total waste.

## *Imani*

Having a celestial being in her purse is even better than a phone, because all she has to do is ask how everyone is doing, and the being will say, "Hendrick's good. He's watching *Goodfellas* with the main Marv. Marv isn't a big crime film guy, but he's enjoying himself all right. Let's see. Kennedy's working on some essay about the industrial revolution. It seems well written, as far as I can tell, though academic writing isn't my thing. Hmm. Tomas is drawing a two-headed tortoise with missile launchers attached to his shell. Everyone's giving off a nice, blue aura, so no one's getting sick or anything. That's about it, I guess."

At any point throughout the day, Imani can go into the bathroom at work and ask for updates like this. She still feels somewhat anxious every time she hears the helper speaking to her, but she expects she'll get used to everything soon. As Marv always says, "There's a very fine line between being awestruck and frightened."

Five minutes from home, Imani says, "Can you have the other helpers tell the kids to come downstairs? I need help with these groceries."

From inside her open purse, the helper says, "Well, I can't exactly contact the other helpers directly. Since we're, you know, spiritual beings, we all have certain mental defenses. I can relay the message directly to the kids, though."

"I see." The hairs on Imani's arms rise. "So, you can speak directly into their minds?"

"In a way."

For a moment, Imani feels like reaching into her purse and crushing the helper in her hand. The feeling quickly passes, however. Like Marv told her, her mind will want to reject this new way of existence, the same way the Luddites of the nineteenth century feared and destroyed weaving machinery. The same way some older people refuse to use the internet. But she has nothing whatso-ever to fear in these helpers. For years, she's been prepar-ing for their arrival, both mentally and spiritually. She's ready.

Once she parks her SUV in the driveway, her children come out of the house and help with the grocery bags.

"Sweetie," Imani says, touching her son's shoulder. "How are you? Are you okay with the helpers being here?"

"Yeah," he says. "He can make my drawings 3-D."

Inside the house, she finds Marv and her husband side-by-side on the couch, both dressed in *Star Trek* shirts and sweatpants, looking as twin-like as ever. The big difference between them is that Hendrick seems en-raptured by the movie they're watching, and Marv's slouched back with his eyes closed.

"I left you something in the bedroom," Hendrick says.

"What is it?" Imani says.

"You'll see."

After putting away most of the groceries, Imani carries the remaining bag with her upstairs. Inside her own bedroom, she finds a peanut bobblehead waiting for her, in the spot where the grinning porcelain peanut used to stand. She smiles, and a mild warmth diffuses throughout her chest, and then she worries that Hendrick's only doing this because he feels guilty about something.

"Stop it," she says.

In Marv's room, she empties the fabric bag of Gatorade bottles onto his bed and begins lining them up on the windowsill, the way that he likes. Apparently, as a child, Marv would carry bottles and cans into his bedroom and stack them into pyramids. He's never stopped wanting his bottles close.

While she's reaching for another Gatorade, she notices a crinkled piece of paper on the bed, and she recognizes Hendrick's handwriting. She knows she shouldn't read the note, whatever it is, but she spots her name written in sharp, slapdash letters. She flattens out the note, but she doesn't actually remove the paper from off the bed.

The note is a bulleted list that says:

- 17 years ago. The first time I kissed Imani. We were standing outside that Mexican food stand with the pineapple drink she likes. She said the cold air was making her say burrrrrr . . . ito. When I realized she was actually cold, I gave her my jacket, and she kissed me.

- 16 and a half years ago, perhaps? We were at the beach, walking on these smooth, black rocks, and Imani kept answering my questions with one-word responses. Back then she would talk my damn ear off any chance she got, so I was surprised she was so quiet. I asked her what was wrong, and then she cried. I'd seen her cry before, but not like this. Usually, I feel a bit uncomfortable around people when they cry, but I felt this strong impulse to protect her from whatever it was that was making her so sad. I felt protective in a way that I didn't even know existed before that day.

- About 15 years ago, I believe. We were still living in the apartment at this point, and Kennedy wasn't born yet. I rarely ever get ill, but I was sick as all hell. Germs freak her out, but she still came into the bedroom and picked up my used Kleenex like they were nothing. Whenever she came into the bedroom, she would make these silly faces at me that

Imani assumes there's more writing on the back of the paper, but she doesn't flip the sheet over to find out. She stares at the note for a while longer, not reading any of the words. Years and years ago, Hendrick would write silly poems for her and leave them inside her purse or a pocket for her to find. Is this note a skeleton of a new stupid poem? Is the note on Marv's bed because Hendrick wants his brother's advice?

Maybe the peanut bobblehead and the poem are a good sign. Maybe Hendrick's sensed the rift between Imani and himself, and he simply wants to try harder. Imani doesn't know if the helpers are responsible for Hendrick's sudden interest in romance, or if her husband's leading the charge himself. Ultimately, she doesn't really care either way.

When she goes downstairs, she makes a silly face at Hendrick from across the living room. He doesn't laugh at her, or grin, or throw a pillow. But he does smile at her a little before turning to the TV again. That's something, though, isn't it? Maybe, for now, that's enough.

# TUESDAY

## *Tomas*

Everest doesn't bother Tomas at all during first recess, but during second recess, the bully balances on the cement ring and flicks Tomas three times on the top of the head. He says, "Hey, Spot," after each attack. And then, after he's done, Everest says, "Mark says your mom drinks pee and that's why you have weird marks. Your mom probably drinks pee every night."

"She doesn't," Tomas whispers.

"Yeah, she does." He flicks his head one more time and then hops off the cement.

After Everest's long gone, Little Uncle Marv says, "Can I have some more of that Slim Jim?"

"We're not supposed to eat at recess," Tomas says.

"Please. I'm starving."

Tomas sets his pencil down and transfers a chunk of Slim Jim from the big part of his backpack to the small pocket in front. While the helper chomps noisily at the meat, the boy continues working on the demonic elephant with a fiery serpent for a trunk. He touches his mechanical pencil to the paper, but he can't see the elephant's face in his mind anymore. He can only see Everest, and his spiky blond hair, and his cornflower-blue eyes.

Tomas closes his eyes then so he can take himself to that first time he visited his Uncle Marv's studio. For a while, he can see the papier-mâché T. rex and the taxidermied crow with the googly eyes and the sea serpent wrapped around a child's leg. But then he's thinking about Everest again. He's thinking about the first time Everest flicked him during class, when Mrs. Williams wasn't looking. Tomas's body froze in place, and his whole face heated up. Everest whispered something behind him, but Tomas couldn't hear the words. Right then, Mrs. Williams asked for the answer, and everyone in the class said, "Seven," except for Tomas.

Tomas opens his eyes again when Little Uncle Marv says, "That Everest kid really is a piece of work. I've probed his mind a bit, and he has all the makings of a cold-blooded dictator. I'm not kidding. But like I said before, all he needs is a little enlightenment. Invite him to our house, and your uncle can make him stop picking on you."

Tomas looks again at his half-finished elephant, but his mind goes to another time in the classroom, when

Everest managed to flick his stomach with two fingers. He remembers a time in the hallway when Everest said, "You shitter," and squeezed his nose, hard. The memories burst inside him faster. He can smell the citrine-colored pizza in the cafeteria and he can hear the girl vomiting on the handball court and he can feel Everest flicking his neck in the hallway.

"Don't you want him to stop?" Little Uncle Marv says, in the here and now. And suddenly, Tomas feels himself planted deep inside the present again.

"Yeah," Tomas says, looking at the white space where his elephant's head should be.

"Good." Little Uncle Marv chews loudly on the Slim Jim for a few seconds. "Then I need you to man up, like your dad always says. Man up, and march over there, and ask that little douchebag to your house. I'll be there with you the whole time. If he tries anything, I'll let him have it."

"What if he doesn't want to come to the house?"

"Well, try anyway. Let's get the thought planted in his head and work our way from there."

After putting away his drawing notebook, Tomas considers abandoning the plan and playing some handball instead. But as soon as he looks at the handball court, his memories explode inside him again, faster than before. He smells the vomit and hears the vomiting and feels the flicks on his ears and his throat and his eyelid.

Tomas walks toward the soccer field, staring at the blacktop, holding his breath.

"You'll be fine," Little Uncle Marv says, from inside the backpack. "I'll protect you."

Everest and Mark both stand up as soon as Tomas reaches his destination. They're each holding small sticks, about the size of a pencil.

Tomas releases his breath finally and says, "Do you want to play at my house?"

"He wants you to play at his pee house," Mark says, tapping his stick against his crotch.

"I don't go to pee houses," Everest says. "Your mom would probably want to drink all my pee."

"It's not a pee house," Tomas says, because he's not sure what else to say at this point. He doesn't know how to convince a boy like Everest to go anywhere, or to do anything. Boys like Everest remind Tomas of the time he tumbled over and over under a wave. No matter what Tomas did, the wave wouldn't stop.

Everest reaches out to flick Tomas again, only this time his hand stops partway, and the boy collapses to the grass, screaming. The bully covers his face with his hands. Tomas can see a patch of urine spreading across the boy's jeans.

Tomas expects Mark to say something or do something, but he only stands there in silence, staring down at his friend. At the sight of a yard duty running in their direction, Tomas walks away, back toward his tree.

"Was that your powers?" Tomas says.

"Yeah," Little Uncle Marv says. "I made him remember this duck that . . . well, let's just say he's had a taste of how powerful we are. I know it seems like he'd be too afraid to come over to your house now, but that's because you're looking at all this from your own viewpoint. You don't understand boys like Everest. I do. He's almost at the point now where he'll say yes."

Tomas doesn't understand any of that, but he nods anyway.

Back in the classroom, the school day goes on as usual until Little Uncle Marv speaks up during silent reading time. "Put me on your desk," he says. "Hurry."

"This is quiet time," Mrs. Williams says from behind her desk.

"Put me on your desk," Little Marv says again. "If we don't do this now, Everest will torment you forever."

At the mention of Everest's name, Tomas feels the memories bombarding him again. Pizza, vomit, flick, flick, flick. He jumps from memory to memory, all over the school, feeling the sharp jabs of pain.

Quickly, Tomas unzips his backpack and places Little Marv on his desk.

"Hey, look at me!" Little Marv says, performing an awkward jig on the desk. "I'm a weird little creature! Look over here!"

"Look!" Amanda says, pointing.

A few of his classmates scream, with either delight or fear; Tomas isn't sure which.

"What is that?" Pablo says.

"I'm a weird little guy!" Little Uncle Marv says, doing the dance Pee-wee Herman does in the movie.

Tomas notices Mrs. Williams standing nearby now, with her hand over her mouth. The boy wants to explain to her that Little Marv is a helper sent here from another dimension, but before he can even attempt that, Mrs. Williams falls forward, hitting her head on Amanda's desk on the way down. Amanda screams. Tomas screams with her. All around him, the boy's classmates faint, slapping their heads on their desks. Pablo, who stood moments ago, crumples to the grayish-blue carpet.

Tomas opens his mouth to speak, but no words want to come out.

"Don't worry," Little Uncle Marv says, no longer dancing. "They're all fine. Mrs. Williams might need to ice her head for a while, but it's not a concussion."

Tomas looks around the classroom and notices the only other person who didn't faint.

"Hey, Everest," Little Uncle Marv says. "If you come to

play, Tomas will give you a creature just like me. All you have to do is accept the invitation."

Everest doesn't respond. He only sits there, staring at Little Uncle Marv, with his head tilted to the side.

"Okay, put me back," the helper says.

After Tomas zips up his backpack again, Mrs. Williams and the other kids wake up, and they don't say anything about Little Uncle Marv or his little dance. Mrs. Williams says she slipped. She apologizes for scaring everyone.

Tomas doesn't believe for a minute that Everest will come to his house to play after everything that happened. But then, after the final bell rings, the bully walks over and hands Tomas a piece of paper.

"That's my phone number," Everest says. "I'll come over, if I can really have one."

"You can," Little Marv says, from inside the backpack.

Everest walks away then without flicking Tomas even once. As Tomas heads for the bus, he does feel a little safer and a little stronger. But, in spite of this, the boy doesn't want to team up with the helper anymore. He can't stop thinking about the *thunk* of Mrs. Williams's head hitting the desk and the image of Pablo collapsing to the carpet like a dropped marionette. Tomas doesn't want Everest to come over, but he doesn't tell Little Uncle Marv that. He's sure that the helper would only tell him to man up and fight his fears again. So, Tomas continues his work on the demonic elephant, and he tries unsuccessfully to push Everest and all the Uncle Marvs out of his mind. He wonders what will happen tonight. He's not sure what Little Uncle Marv meant by *enlightenment,* but whatever it is, he hopes it won't make Everest scream and pee his pants again.

## Hendrick

As the monster promised, Hendrick feels hardly any apprehension today, calling up Cupcake and Kandi and Ambyr and another Cupcake. Apparently, the imp can't change a woman's voice the way he can change her appearance, so Hendrick decides to keep calling up escorts until he finds one with an appropriately raspy voice. In the end, he decides on the second Cupcake even though her voice isn't quite as deep as Morgaine's.

After the call, Hendrick spends a few minutes throwing away Brett's water bottles and granola wrappers and moldy baby carrots. There's little he despises more than picking up after another person, but then again, he doesn't want his experience today to be marred by the sight and smell of trash.

"Do you have any food in here?" the creature says, standing and stretching on the pool table. "I'm dying."

Hendrick uses a tissue to drop a half-eaten hard-boiled egg into the trash. "There's some Peanut Butter Apocalypse in the freezer."

"Nah, I told you already, Hen. I need meat." He kicks at the eight ball. "And keep in mind, if I'm starving, I won't be able to concentrate on the glamour."

Hendrick sighs and finds some slightly expired slices of organic turkey bologna in the fridge. While the imp dives into the meat, Hendrick plays a little more of the new video game he bought at the murder mall. In the game, he visits alien planets and hunts giant aliens with gnarled tusks and luminescent hides. After finishing one off, he can take a picture with his kill and transmit the photo back home to Earth. The rhinoceros-like creature he's electrocuting ends up crushing his skull with a cloven foot.

With his mouth full, the imp says, "You know, this turkey bologna tastes just like regular bologna. I'm impressed. Not that I've actually eaten regular bologna, I guess, but I can still access your brother's memory of eating bologna. There's no real difference, really."

"Uh-huh." Hendrick does appreciate everything the imp's doing for him, but at the same time he wishes the creature wouldn't talk so much. If Hendrick wanted to talk to a Marvin-like person, he'd chat with his actual brother instead of one of these half-assed facsimiles.

About ten minutes later than she promised, Cupcake arrives in a little black dress and high heels.

"Hi there," she says. "This is a nice place."

Her voice sounds less raspy than she did on the phone. Hendrick feels a tinge of anger about that, but he decides to move on and hope for the best. He glances over at the imp, who's standing perfectly still on top of a bookshelf, not even blinking his eyes. What must be a hunk of balogna dangles from his chin.

Cupcake brushes her fingers against Hendrick's arm and says, "What do you say we finish the business side of things first. Then we can focus all our attention on all the good parts."

"Sure," Hendrick says. Cold sweat dribbles down his back while he retrieves the envelope of hundreds from his messenger bag.

She takes the envelope that Hendrick took from Imani's stationery drawer early in the morning. "Let me go freshen up," she says. "And then we can discuss exactly what you want from our time together."

As soon as Cupcake disappears into the bathroom, Hendrick turns to the imp and says, "You said you could change her."

"Give me a fucking minute," the creature says, peeling the bologna from his chin.

Hendrick supposes that Cupcake only went into the

bathroom to count the money, because she doesn't even flush the toilet before coming back.

"Okay, tell me what you want," she says.

Sitting next to her on the bed, Hendrick explains the scenario he desires. Eventually, her face becomes shrouded by a smear of soft colors. And then Morgaine's sitting there across from him in a black velvet dress. She gazes into him with dark emerald eyes. He can see the slit of her pink tongue between her barely open lips.

Only moments ago, Hendrick asked her to strip for him before ever touching his body, but he changes his mind. He crawls closer to her. He holds her and kisses her, and even though sweat's running down his back, he feels more excited than anything else. He can do this.

"You're in my complete control," she says, the way he told her. "You have to do everything I say."

Soon after he removes her dress, one of her eyes changes from green to brown and her mouth becomes a jagged line of crimson red. Her nose blurs and then disappears completely.

"Shit," Hendrick says. "I'll be right back."

"Okay," she says, and one of her eyes flips upside-down.

After snatching the imp from off the bookshelf, he storms into the bathroom. "You did that on purpose, didn't you?" he says, squeezing the monster in his hand.

"You're fucking with me."

"I'm not," the creature says, trying to squirm himself free. "I swear to fucking God I'm not. Can you stop crushing me and let me explain? Jeez."

Hendrick loosens his grip, but only a little.

"Everything was going fine," the creature says. "But then, all of a sudden, Marv left. His presence, I mean. His energy. And the thing is, I can't handle this level of glamour by myself. I need Marv's power to flow through me. So, if we just wait a minute, I'm sure Marv's energy will come back, and then we can finish up here."

Hendrick doesn't understand what the fuck the monster's talking about, and he doesn't particularly care to find out.

After what feels like an eternity, the imp says, "Okay, he's back. She's Morgaine again."

"If you fuck this up again, I might crush you for real next time."

"Marv won't like you threatening me like that."

Hendrick snickers and returns the creature to the top of the bookshelf.

Back in bed, Hendrick says, "Sorry about that."

"Don't worry about it, sweetie," Morgaine says, her face whole and perfect. "Now you're under my command. I need you to obey me."

And Hendrick obeys. At first, he feels somewhat shy

and awkward, but never once does he suffer any unbear-able guilt. In fact, he hardly thinks of Imani at all. What-ever he used to feel for Imani seems to be blurred over, thanks to the imp.

Last night, the creature said that all those favorite memories he wrote down could be returned to Hendrick whenever he's ready, but he thinks perhaps he'll leave them buried after all. He doesn't want those ancient, bar-ren feelings to hold him back anymore. Morgaine, he's decided, is only the beginning.

## Kennedy

Kennedy wants to pay attention to Ms. Withers's lecture on the Salem Witch Trials, but how are you supposed to concentrate with an i forgive u text on your phone. Alejandra even punctuated the sentence with six daisy emojis and a heart. Every so often, Kennedy can't help but glance down at the screen on her lap.

"The trials left twenty-four innocent people dead," Ms. Withers says, writing a large 24 on the marker board in green letters. "Two dogs were hanged as well."

Sitting near Kennedy, Alika gasps at the mention of the dogs and then raises her hand. When she's called on, Alika says, "Why did they kill the dogs?"

"I don't know the specifics," Ms. Withers says. "But I believe they were executed as suspected accomplices of the so-called witches."

"Dogs would never do that," Alika says, quietly.

At this point, Kennedy hears Fantastico whispering incomprehensibly from under her desk. The two of them aren't supposed to speak in a crowded room like this, so the teenager assumes this must be some sort of emergency. She drops her penguin pen onto the floor and when she leans down, she listens carefully.

"Ask to go to the bathroom," Fantastico whispers. "Hurry."

Once Kennedy retrieves the bathroom key attached to a miniature toilet seat, she heads outside. A surge of wind blows the raindrops slantwise, into the sanctuary of the overhang. Kennedy's never minded getting wet, though.

Before they even reach the bathroom, Fantastico says, "I don't know how much time we have, Ken, so I need you to just listen to me, and then do what I tell you." His voice sounds higher than usual, and his words sometimes crack in the middle. "Marv, he . . . he's not your uncle. He's not your spiritual guru. He's only been in your life for a few days."

Kennedy laughs.

"I'm not kidding around here!" Fantastico says. "He's observed and fucked with your short-term memories constantly, and at the same time he's pushed himself backwards through your long-term, tweaking with shit, implanting himself all over the place. He still hasn't rooted himself deeply in the beginning moments of your existence. And once he does, well, I don't even want to say how he could mold you then. I mean, I get that none of this makes any sense to you. But the point is, Marvin is not your friend. I'm not your friend. You and your family, you're going to end up imprisoned or dead or worse, like all the others."

Sitting in the bathroom stall, Kennedy removes Fantastico from her backpack and places him on the boxy toilet-roll holder. He taps at his chin, again and again.

"You have to squish me," he says, and he vomits a little. "Or twist my head off, or whatever you want."

"I can't do that," Kennedy says. "I would never—"

"I get that you're a nice person and all, and you don't want to kill anyone. But seriously, I'm barely alive. I'm random bits and pieces of Marv's personality all mashed together into a carbon-based antenna. I'm just a conduit of his power. And you need to crush me now and stay the fuck away from Marv and all the other little Marvs. You can't let them find you. Otherwise, they'll suck you back into all this."

Using a square of toilet paper, Kennedy wipes the vomit off her helper's flaming-skull shirt. She can feel hot tears building up inside her. "I don't want to hurt you," she says.

Fantastico rubs at his temples with both index fingers. "There's no time to argue about this. Usually, when Marvin's energy is inside me, I have to act in ways that would benefit him somehow. But right now, he's passed out or something, and he can't define the trajectory of my existence. What I'm saying is, this is my chance to help you. Probably my one and only. If Marvin comes back, he'll have control of me again and you'll forget all of this. Please, Kennedy. You have to do it."

The teenager shakes her head. "I won't."

"Well, fuck. I don't know what else to do. Sorry I didn't come up with a better plan. I really didn't want you to . . . to end up like the others."

The teenager wipes a tear from off her cheek. "I don't really understand what you said or anything, but maybe you could tell my mom. She'll know what to do."

"Yeah," he says, slowly. "I shouldn't have put this on you. Sometimes, I forget you're just a kid. I need to talk to your mom." Fantastico closes his eyes then and taps at his chin, fast. He mouths a few words silently, but she can't read his lips. When he opens his eyes again, he says, "Shit, he's back."

For a moment, the world whirls around Kennedy, as if she's spinning fast on a roundabout, the way she did when she was younger. When reality rights itself again, she says, "What did you want to talk with me about?"

Fantastico sighs and says, "Nothing. Go back to class."

The teenager doesn't understand why her helper seemed so adamant about getting her out here if he didn't have anything to say. Then again, she's in too good a mood to waste her time chastising a celestial being. So, she lets the subject go.

Back in the classroom, Kennedy lets herself look at Alejandra's text once every ten minutes, and she only breaks her rule a couple times.

Her good mood follows her throughout the day. By the time she steps inside her house, she's once again fully confident that she and Alejandra will move to Los Angeles someday and become a singer-songwriter duo and open a sanctuary for orphaned kittens.

Despite the warm temperature in the house, Kennedy shivers a little walking up the stairs. Right as she enters the hallway, Uncle Marv says, "Hey, Kennedy! Can you come in here? Oh, and can you get your brother first? Bring both your helpers."

"Here we go," Fantastico says, inside her backpack.

Kennedy expects Uncle Marv to lead her and her brother in another meditation session, but this time, he doesn't tell her to get comfortable on the rug. This time, he sits on the edge of the bed, staring down at the curled hands on his lap.

"I need your helpers for a minute," he says, quietly.

Kennedy and Tomas hand over the celestial beings and then sit together on the rug.

"Fantastico," he says, staring at the helper in his right hand. "You tried to fuck me over, but hey, I get it. You care about the girl and you were being protective. I wasn't inside you at the time, so of course you're going to rebel a little when you get the chance." Uncle Marv tilts his head to the side, and Fantastico mimics the action. "I'm going to forgive you for all the crap you pulled, but you need to tell me if you tinkered with anyone's memories while I was out of you. At the end of your conversation with Ken, you said you should talk to her mom. Did you mess with Imani at all?"

"I don't know," Fantastico says, his voice cracking. "If I did mess with her brain, I made myself forget what I did, so that I couldn't tell you."

"Agh," Uncle Marv says. "Well, could you search her mind for a while and let me know if you find any abnormalities I didn't create myself?"

"Yeah, of course."

Kennedy knows that she heard her Fantastico and her uncle speaking, but now she can't remember a single word that was said. When she opens her mouth to ask Uncle Marv a question, she can't recall what it is she wanted to say.

"As for you," Uncle Marv says, lifting up Tomas's

helper now. "You showed yourself to an entire classroom. That kind of spectacle is against the rules for a reason, you know? We had to rewrite all their memories all at once, and you sapped my energy dry. I passed the fuck out."

Tomas's helper spits up and says, "I was trying to help you, Marvin. And how was I supposed to know you couldn't handle a room full of kids? You used to be stronger than this."

"You're careless," Uncle Marv says. "And you're cruel. Tomas is one of my people, but you bashed his teacher's head against the desk. You scared him half to death. I get that you were trying to act in my best interests, but I think you're defective."

"Oh, fuck you." Tomas's helper squirms in the man's hand. "I'm as much a part of you as all the others. I'm only cruel because you—"

The helper's small head pops in an eruption of clear liquid that runs down Uncle Marv's hand. Marv tosses the dead helper onto the rug and says, "Hey, don't worry, Tomas. We have a couple spare."

Kennedy turns to her brother, but she only sees his wide eyes for a moment before darkness closes in on her from all sides. When she wakes up again, she doesn't feel quite as refreshed as she usually does after a meditation session. She stands up and notices that her brother's already gone. As for Uncle Marv, he's sitting cross-legged on the bed, his hand inside the Amazon box again. Fantastico's sitting on the pillow beside him, his eyes only half-open.

"I fell asleep," she says, stretching.

"Yeah," Uncle Marv says, not looking in her direction. "Well, that's enough spiritual advancement for the day. You have a lot of homework to do, don't you?"

"Yeah." Kennedy picks up Fantastico and carries him carefully to her room. Despite her slow movements, he still vomits after she places him on her desk. He won't take his eyes off his hands.

"Are you all right?" Kennedy says.

"Yeah," he says. "I'm good."

But he doesn't sound good. He sounds as if the world's about to end. Kennedy doesn't have any time to deal with apocalypses right now, though, because she needs to finish a couple hours of work before dinner.

Working on Ms. Withers's assignment, Kennedy thinks about how all the women who lied and said they were witches were allowed to live, and all the women who told the truth and said they weren't witches were killed. Kennedy pictures herself wearing a gray gown and long woolen stockings and a close-fitting coif to cover her hair. She imagines someone stripping off her layers of petticoats to see if she has any moles or birthmarks or third nipples. She supposes, if Tomas were alive during the trials, he would have been considered a witch because of his vitiligo. They probably would have killed him.

"Do you know about the Salem Witch Trials?" Kennedy says.

"Yeah," Fantastico says, lying on his marble coaster, staring up at the ceiling. "I mean, I watched that *Crucible* movie a few years ago. A little too serious for my tastes."

"I just don't get why stuff like that happens. There's the witch trials and the Spanish Inquisition and all of that. They keep killing people for such stupid reasons. Why do people do that?"

"Hmm." Fantastico sits up and looks into her eyes. "I can read that textbook of yours through your memories, and the author talks a lot about the hysteria and the fear and the religious zealotry. But that's overcomplicating everything, you know? What he really needs to write about are those judges, those men who liked killing people. They gave all sorts of excuses for their killing and torturing and transgressing, but that's all they were. Excuses. When you're dealing with people who like to kill, things will eventually go to shit."

Fantastico lies back on his coaster again and closes his eyes. After considering his answer to her question, Kennedy decides to change the last couple paragraphs in her assignment. She writes about the judges and their bloodlust, and partway through a sentence, she feels as if someone's staring at her back. She trembles in her chair, and she feels stupid for doing so. There's no one there. There's no Puritanical judge back from the dead, out to hang her for the moles on her back. She glances once behind her, just to make sure. And, of course, there's no one there, but despite the silly relief she should be feeling, she doesn't feel any less afraid.

## Imani

Hendrick was supposed to be home an hour and fifteen minutes ago, and he's not responding to any of her texts. On the one hand, Imani's afraid that a speeding Silverado smashed into her husband while he was trying to cross the street. She can see his mangled body with an arm twisted backward, and cracked bones poking out of his skin.

On the other hand, she's furious that tonight is Hendrick's turn to cook, and yet she's the one dumping dinosaur macaroni into the boiling water. In truth, she knows Hendrick's probably not dead or dying. He's probably working late again, and he hasn't once thought to check his phone for texts.

To decorate the table for Dino Din, Imani searches a high

cabinet for a few pterodactyl eggs (which are actually hollowed-out ostrich eggs she found at an antique mall) and displays them inside a dinosaur-themed salad bowl. She wonders how long her kids will put up with her themed dinners. She hopes she has a few years left, at least.

Sitting on Imani's place mat, her helper says, "Hey, Im, I don't mean to worry you, but some guy tried to grab Kennedy on the street recently."

"What?" Imani says, freezing with a pan in her hand.

"Don't worry; her helper protected her. But I'm a little concerned about the guy. I'm afraid he'll go after Kennedy again, or someone like her. Now, I'm not a hundred percent sure or anything, but I think with your help, we could stop him."

"What do you mean?" Imani says.

Her helper picks at a loose string coming out of his sleeveless denim shirt. "Well, what we need to do is get the guy here. That way, the main Marv can help him reach a state of enlightenment, and then he won't be any trouble to anybody. The difficult part will be finding the guy. Kennedy's helper didn't get a super deep look inside his mind, but the helper did manage to suss out that the guy seems to be a creature of routine. I'm guessing if we go out there at the same time of day he tried to grab Kennedy, there's a good chance we'll see him. Then it's only a matter of convincing him to come over."

"I don't want a man like that in my house," Imani says, setting the plate on the table.

"Yeah, I get that. Just promise me you'll think it over."

"Okay." Despite her promise, Imani knows that she'll never agree to allowing a man like that in her home. If Marvin wants to go find the guy and enlighten his mind, then he should do that and leave the family out of it.

While she's cutting out the brontosaurus-shaped cookies, she finally hears the front door open. She washes her hands and walks into the living room. "You're late," she says. "You could have texted me."

"Sorry," he says, but he doesn't sound sorry. He doesn't give her his usual kiss on the side of her mouth. He doesn't even look at her. "Marvin needs me upstairs."

"Can you at least help me set the table first?" she says.

But her husband heads upstairs without so much as a glance over his shoulder. After standing in the living room for a few seconds, Imani decides not to follow him. She's feeling especially anxious at the moment, and she's in no mood for a big argument.

When Tomas's friend finally arrives, Imani yells upstairs for her son but he doesn't appear.

"He must have his headphones on," Imani says. "I'll go get him in a minute."

For a few minutes, Imani chats with Everest's mother, who only seems interested in talking about local traffic conditions. Somehow, Imani manages to keep a smile plastered on her face the whole time.

Once the mother leaves, Imani approaches Everest and says, "Can I get you anything?"

He glances up from his small tablet, with his Nikes on the ottoman. "My mom said you were making macaroni."

"Yes, sweetie, but do you want anything before dinner? Can I get you a drink? Orange juice?"

"No."

At this point, Tomas descends the stairs and stands close to his mother.

"Why don't you two go play outside," Imani says. "I'll let you know when dinner's ready."

The two boys look at each other and then march outside in silence. Tomas isn't the most sociable kid in the universe, so Imani's somewhat surprised that he'd invite someone over beyond Pablo. She's proud of her son for branching out.

Continuing the preparations for Dino Din, she thinks about that look Hendrick gave her when he first got home. He's seemed distant before, but never quite like this.

Back when she was a kid, Imani would tell herself that if she cleaned the house perfectly, if she cooked her mother's dinner perfectly, then everything would be all right. And right now, even though she hates herself for thinking it, she tells herself the same thing. *Prepare everything just right and your world might not fall apart. Maybe he'll still love you, after all.*

## Tomas

Playing outside with Everest isn't the anarchic nightmare that Tomas expects. There's no flicking. There aren't even any insults. But Tomas isn't at ease. He fears that at any moment, the bully will wander off and find the entrance to the tunnel. Tomas doesn't think Everest could cause any permanent damage to the courtyard, but Tomas doesn't want him there, anyway. In the end, the worst thing that Everest does is intentionally dribble the basketball in a few puddles so that he can get Tomas wet.

They only play for a few minutes before they're called in for Dino Dinner. Once they sit down, Tomas's mom says, "Okay, dig in, everyone. Here's the chips and seven-layer diplodocus. And for the meat-eaters among us, here's some Jurassic pork."

"Mom, no," Kennedy says, squishing her own cheeks together with both hands.

"We should have tri-tip next time," their mom continues. "Then I could say tri-tip-ceratops."

"Mom."

Once they dig in, Everest points a fork at the pterodactyl eggs in the middle of the table. Then he leans over to Tomas and says, "Is that where the creatures come from?"

"No," Tomas says.

When Everest reaches for one of the eggs, Tomas drops his fork, knowing that the bully will crush the object in his hands. He'll say, "Sorry," like he does at school when he breaks the chalk in half, but he won't really mean it.

"Be careful with those," Tomas's mom says, just in time, and Everest quickly pulls his hand away.

Freeing his held breath, Tomas picks up his fork again. He pokes at his Jurassic pork. Usually, during Dino Din, his mother will repeat her infamous pterodactyl joke or she'll ask Tomas what he thinks various dinosaurs sound like. "I am an allosaurus," he'll say, in a deepish, gravelly voice. This evening, though, his mother spends much of her time staring down at her plate. Even Kennedy barely says a word. Tomas usually enjoys the quiet, but the silence at this table feels heavy and palpable, like a dark mist suddenly filling the room.

When Tomas looks across the table, his uncle gives him a brisk thumbs-up, using his hand that's resting beside his plate. Uncle Marv smiles in a way that makes his face almost unrecognizable. Generally, his uncle only displays a slight, lopsided smirk. Now he grins broadly, stretching his lips far across his face.

Tomas knows that his uncle's proud of him for facing his bully and his fears. He knows that his father wants to take him to Thomas's Bar & Grill to celebrate what the boy's accomplishing today. But right now, Tomas doesn't care about any of that. Now all he wants is to get this dinner over with so that Everest can go back home, far away from the puddles and the courtyard and the pterodactyl eggs.

Thankfully, Kennedy breaks through the silence with some information about the Salem Witch Trials. Tomas listens carefully until she talks about how the men hanged two dogs. Then he tries his best not to listen anymore.

After Dino Din winds down, Uncle Marv says, "Hey, did I tell you guys I finally finished my new project? Maybe I should give Tomas the first look, since he contributed a bunch of the drawings." He looks at Tomas now, still smiling like before. "Your friend can come too, if he likes."

"Go ahead, boys," Tomas's mom says.

And so, Uncle Marv leads the way upstairs, into his room. He sets the cardboard box on his bed, so that the diorama is facing the boys. Tomas peers into a small, cluttered room with burgundy brick walls and a tan floor. Of course, Tomas recognizes his potbelly stove and his dress form and his industrial sewing machine table. Like before, the drawings become hazy for a moment and then swell into three-dimensional objects. Black smoke spirals upward from the stove, and the tiny sewing machine needle moves up and down. Carefully, Uncle Marv sets three Tiny Uncle Marvs into the box. The three tiny uncles are wearing different clothes from the usual helpers, so they must be the extra ones who always stay in Uncle Marv's room.

"So," Uncle Marv says, tapping the top of the box with a finger. "This is based on a scene from *The Garbage Pail Kids Movie*. These guys aren't the best singers in the world, but they have been practicing fairly faithfully in their free time. Okay, guys. Go ahead."

The Tiny Uncle Marvs clear their throats simultaneously and then begin singing a song about working together. Tomas has never heard this particular song before, but he can tell that they're all off-key. While the Marvs sing, they dance awkwardly around the room. One of them accidentally trips on another Marv's foot and then knocks the potbelly stove over.

When Everest reaches toward the scene, the real Uncle Marv says, "Don't touch them while they're performing."

After the song ends, the helpers bow slightly and Tomas claps.

"Do I get to have one now?" Everest asks.

"Yeah, of course," Uncle Marv says, his finger tapping over and over against the cardboard box. "Hey, Tomas, could you go get your mom for me? I need to ask her something."

Tomas nods and walks out of the room. As soon as he crosses the threshold of the doorway, he hears Everest say, "Let me go. Let me go!"

Tomas quickly turns back, but Uncle Marv's room now blazes with amaranth-colored fire. For a few seconds, some of the flames look a little like arms reaching out to him. Everest screams then, somewhere in the rosy red fire, and the door slams closed.

Rushing downstairs for his mom, Tomas hopes that the enlightenment will be over very soon. He finds his mother in the living room, walking in his direction, with an anguished look on her face.

By the time he reaches her, Tomas can't remember what it is he wanted to say.

"Sweetie, what's wrong?" his mother says, wiping a tear from his cheek.

"Nothing," he says. "I'm gonna trampoline."

Outside, Tomas walks past the trampoline, however, across the stepping stones and through the tunnel. He sits on the wet floor of scarlet and russet and golden bronze. From one jacket pocket he pulls out the bodybuilding mouse and the headless bobblehead and the army man who only fears balloons. From his other jacket pocket he lifts out his helper and sets him on the leaves.

Little Uncle Marv uses his powers to make the mouse's mouth move. "Come on, guys," Little Marv says, syncing his voice with the mouse's mouth movements. "Let's defeat that croc-topus."

"Yeah!" Tomas says, holding the army man.

As the two of them play together, Tomas holds his breath from time to time in order to keep his good luck from abandoning him. Everest's mom said that Everest was too sick to come to Dino Dinner after all, but there's always a chance that the bully's mom will call up again and say that Everest is feeling much better now. She could say he wants to come this evening to play. Tomas takes another deep breath, and for now he feels lucky that he can be here in the courtyard, alone with his helper.

Tomas jumps a little when a crow shrieks from above. When he looks up, he doesn't see the crow, but he notices a branch that looks like an arm with long, outstretched fingers. For some reason, the sight makes him shiver in the back of his neck. But then he turns his attention back to the army man in his hand, and his goosebumps fade away. Whether he's facing a tree monster with gnarled hands or a croc-topus, he has nothing to fear in the courtyard. Here, the heroes always win.

## Hendrick

Most of the time, Hendrick doesn't like to stay in the same room as Imani when she's in one of her moods. She'll skitter from place to place, straightening and scrubbing and reorganizing. And every once in a while, she'll give Hendrick a reproving look, as if he should be straightening and scrubbing and reorganizing along with her. She usually succeeds in making him feel guilty.

But this afternoon, as Imani Swiffers the hardwood floors in the living room, Hendrick feels perfectly at peace. He sits side by side with Marv, watching some strange movie about the Garbage Pail Kids that Marv ordered online. When Hendrick turns his head to look at his wife, he feels as if he's still watching a TV screen. Marv promised that the imp could give him a more carefree life, and so far, the little monster is certainly delivering. Hendrick takes another sip of his Old Fashioned.

"I told you this is a fun movie," Marv says.

"Yeah, it's great," Hendrick lies. But, with the imp's powers flowing through him or whatever the fuck's going on, even this terrible film doesn't have the power to dampen Hendrick's mood.

While Imani's dusting the family photos on the wall, the doorbell rings, twice.

Imani opens the door and a blond woman says, "How

did everything go?" She then steps into the house without being invited in.

"Excuse me?" Imani says.

The woman smiles a little and says, "Was Everest any trouble? If he broke anything, let me know."

"Oh, you're Everest's mom," Imani says, passing her Swiffer from one hand to the other. "On the phone, you said Everest was too sick to come. Why are you—"

Imani finishes her sentence with a gasp, because the blond woman faints and slams her head on the hardwood floor. A moment later, Imani's knees buckle as well, though she doesn't collapse so quickly. She ends up sitting, with the Swiffer still in her hand.

Hendrick himself feels a little dizzy. When he tries to stand up, Marv puts a hand on his shoulder and says, "Hey, don't worry. I'll take care of this."

So, Hendrick stays put and takes a sip of his Old Fashioned. He only feels a minor twinge of guilt for not helping his wife and the big-busted blond woman, but then again, in any kind of emergency, you're much better off letting Marv handle everything. Imani still doesn't seem to understand that, though, because she's staring at him from the floor, giving him one of her most pleading looks. He can't blame her, really. Imani still thinks that Marv is her twin brother. She doesn't understand that he's more than human. He's always watched over Hendrick, and he's never grown a day older. Marv's promised that with his help, Hendrick won't grow any older either.

While Hendrick muses about all this, Marv's standing next to the women, tapping two fingers on his forehead. Eventually, Imani closes her eyes and curls up on the floor.

Reaching into his pocket, Marv pulls out one of his creatures.

"I don't want to go with her," the creature says, looking up at Marv. "She's not even one of our people."

"Sorry," Marv says, and he does sound genuinely remorseful. Placing the spare imp in the blond woman's purse, he says, "Well, try to keep her busy for as long as you can."

"Yeah, I will."

While Marv heads back to the couch, Imani and the blond woman open their eyes and stand. They look confused, but only for a moment.

Rubbing her forehead, the blond woman says, "Thanks again for letting me apologize in person. I had no idea Everest was. . . ." She sighs. "As soon as he's over this bug, I'll bring him over to apologize as well. And if he ever bullies Tomas again, please let me know."

"Thank you," Imani says.

After Everest's mother leaves, Imani picks up the Swiffer and rubs at her head again.

As he observes all of this happening, Hendrick feels a little like he's watching a complex TV show from the middle of the season. But he doesn't care too much, really. He doesn't need to understand. Marv will take care of everything.

## *Kennedy*

Kennedy finished up her Salem assignment before dinner, but the assignment isn't quite done with her yet. As her room darkens with the sunset, the teenager bounces from website to website, scavenging whatever morsels of information stand out to her. She doesn't write the details down, but she sometimes repeats the sentences to herself a few times. She wants to remember all this, so she can tell Alejandra about it later.

On her odyssey, she reads about how Tituba, who helped propel the whole witch hunt with her confession, later retracted every word. She was a slave, and she said her master bullied her. Kennedy reads about how an infant died in prison during the trials, and how someone collected the urine from the bewitched girls in order to harm the witches. She reads about how women were stripped to their undergarments and tied up and thrown in icy water. She reads about men who would stab women with needles, all over their bodies, in order to see if the women were evil.

The jarring sound of shattering glass yanks Kennedy back into reality. She looks down and sees orange juice and pale pink glass shards all over the floor.

"Agh," Fantastico says, standing on her desk. "I was leaning against your cup and, well, I'm really sorry."

"It's okay," Kennedy says.

While she sops up the orange juice with a used bath towel, Fantastico says, "Can you put me down on the floor? I can help."

So, Kennedy uses a washcloth to push the broken glass into a pile, and Fantastico picks shards with his hands. When Kennedy tries to object, the helper tells her that he's fine and that he has thick skin.

After dropping a couple handfuls into the larger pile, Fantastico says, "I . . . I'm sorry I can't do more for you, Ken. I can only pick up the small pieces."

"It's okay, really. It's just a glass."

"Yeah."

Moments later, Kennedy notices a thick, translucent liquid leaking from her friend's hands. "Is that blood?"

"Well, in a sense. But it's fine. I can hardly feel pain."

Kennedy sighs and sprints into the bathroom for one of those poop-themed Band-Aids that her mom insisted on buying. She finds Fantastico still carrying splinters of glass on his outstretched palms.

"Stop that," she says, and lifts him back onto the desk. Using a pair of her crafting scissors, she slices a couple strips off the Band-Aid. The bandages still don't fit exactly, but she wraps up his hands anyway.

While she's finishing up with the glass, her mother comes in and crosses her arms over her chest. "Sweetie, why aren't you using a broom and dustpan?"

"I don't know," Kennedy says. "I thought this would work okay."

Her mom bites at a sparkly purple fingernail and says, "Hmm, I suppose you did do a tea-riffic job. That would work if you were drinking iced tea."

"It was orange juice."

"Well, you win some, you lose some." Her mother walks over and picks up a splinter of glass that managed to flee to a far corner of the room. "I was thinking of going on a quick night stroll. Want to come? Tomas says he will."

"Yeah, sounds good."

Her mother drops the splinter of glass onto the larger pile. "Could you ask your dad and uncle if they want to come? I'm going to change shoes."

Her mother disappears, leaving Kennedy feeling a little concerned. The only time her mom ever wants to hike on a freezing night like tonight is when she's in super anxiety mode.

Downstairs, Kennedy finds two helpers arm-wrestling on the ottoman, grunting. Meanwhile, her dad and uncle sit side by side on the couch, staring at the muted TV. Her father brings a glass to his mouth, and some of the liquid dribbles down his chin. He doesn't seem to mind.

"Do you guys want to come to the haunted trail?" Kennedy says.

"Sorry, kid, I'm stuffed," her uncle says, patting his belly. "If I moved, I think I'd explode, Monty Python–style. Have you seen that sketch?"

"I don't think so," the teenager says.

"He's cheating," one of the helpers says, still wrestling on the ottoman. "You're not supposed to lift your elbow."

"I'm not," the other helper says.

Turning to her father, Kennedy says, "Dad, you want to go? Me and Tomas and Mom are going. Maybe we'll see that ghost woman with the veil this time."

"Sorry, sweetie," her father says. "Marvin needs me here."

Kennedy tries to give him an imploring look, because she knows her mom needs help right now. But he never looks away from the screen. A small smile quivers at the edge of his lips and then disappears.

On the drive to the trail, Kennedy tries to tell Fantastico everything she learned about the trials, but he only responds with frail *hmm*s and *yeah*s. It's obvious he doesn't want to talk, so she gives up after a couple minutes. In the silence that follows, Fantastico stands in the cupholder, staring sometimes straight ahead and sometimes at his bandaged hands. Uncle Marv and the helpers never do reveal much of what they're feeling on their faces, but Kennedy can perceive a sense of melancholy in her helper's behavior. Fantastico usually jumps at a chance to talk with her. He usually watches her from wherever he's positioned. Of course, Kennedy wonders what a celestial being might feel sad or worried about, but for now, she lets her curiosity die. She's too concerned about her mom, and she can't handle any more problems right now.

Kennedy decides that she'll talk with Fantastico later, when she's feeling stronger. For now, though, she turns to the window and watches the world pass by in silhouette.


## Imani


Ever since Dino Dinner ended, Imani felt an almost physically painful urge to leave the house. She even caught herself screaming in her head a few times, the way she used to as a child after one of her mother's tirades. Back then, she sometimes worried that her mother could read her mind, but her mother never mentioned the screams.

Imani's feeling much better now, strolling the flat yet labyrinthine trail through a woodland of ancient oaks and arroyo willow trees and bracken ferns. A flurry of pale, ghostly moths frolic around the old-fashioned lanterns that hang from posts along the way. Tomas walks ahead of her, trying to keep pace with his remote-control car. Ordinarily, her son will attempt to pop a wheelie or loop around posts, but tonight, with his helper riding in the vehicle, he keeps his acrobatic driving to a minimum.

As for Kennedy, she climbs the small boulders that appear at the edge of the trail every few yards. And then she surprises Imani by walking over and holding her hand. It's a ridiculous thought, she knows, but the mother worries that if she says anything, she might startle her daughter away. So, for a while, they walk together in silence.

"Mom," Kennedy says, finally. "You know how I told you about that guy who got like psychic visions from insects?"

"Yeah," Imani says.

"I looked into it more, and he pretty much admitted to making the whole thing up. I thought you should know."

"Well, thanks, sweetie."

In a few minutes, they reach the wooden dock that floats over the pond. Imani and her children peek over the edge, and even though they never see the giant catfish at night, they still search the dark waters for him. Kennedy holds her helper over the rail so that he can look as well.

"Don't drop him," Imani says.

"I won't, Mom."

Once they turn away from the water, Tomas's helper says, "Hey, could you carry me for a while? I'm getting carsick in that thing and I don't want to vomit all my innards out."

So, Tomas deposits the helper into his jacket and places an army man in the driver's seat instead.

On nights like tonight, when Imani's feeling overly anxious about her marriage or her life, she likes to walk to the very end of the lighted path. She doesn't actually believe that there's any magic to the ritual, but she tells herself that as soon as she reaches the end of the path, she'll feel stronger. Strong enough to face tomorrow, at least.

Placing her palm on that final lantern post tonight, she feels like that scared, superstitious girl she used to be. But she doesn't mind that much. She stands still for a while, gazing into the darkness, and she imagines that her mother is out there with the veiled woman and the winged coyote and all the other ghosts who supposedly haunt this place. Imani takes a deep breath, feeling grateful that she doesn't have to continue on until the light fades away. She can turn back and go back home.

"Mom," Tomas says, touching her arm.

Imani forgets her mother's ghost and turns to her son. He's sniffling and trembling. Tears sparkle in his eyes.

"What is it, sweetie?" Imani says.

"Uncle Marv," Tomas says. "Uncle Marv gave me a message. He said you have to kill the helpers right now, or me and Kennedy will die. He said to hurry. He said you can't wait even a second."

Without thinking, Imani reaches into her coat pocket and wraps her fingers around her helper. Her mind races. Her body tilts with vertigo. On one side of her consciousness, she feels the weight of all Marv's lectures over the years, instructing her that her family needs the helpers more than anything and anyone. And on the other side blares this new, nebulous warning that her children could die. Imani doesn't know if Tomas is telling the truth. What if killing the helpers would ruin everything, the way Marv has always implied? The two conflicting Marvins shout simultaneously inside her, telling her to kill the helpers and telling her not to. She doesn't know which voice to believe, so ultimately, she decides to trust in her own.

## *Tomas*

Every so often, Tomas likes to take a break from the wheelies and the 360-degree spins so that he can search the darkened chaparral for gleaming coquelicot eyes. Kennedy always says there aren't any real ghosts in this forest, but Tomas hopes to befriend the winged coyote who soars from branch to branch. He imagines himself fusing with the coyote, like the boy and the wolf in Uncle Marv's campfire story. Tomas imagines himself leaping from tree to tree, his eyes burning white like little full moons.

Tomas doesn't believe he would actually like fusing with a ghost in real life, but he wouldn't mind seeing the coyote for a moment. As for the veiled woman, he doesn't want to see her at all. Whenever he thinks about her too much during the hike, he has to move closer to his mom.

Once they reach the end of the illuminated section, his mom puts her hand on the last post, like she always does. Tomas knows that she's going to take some time to stare at the shadowy trail ahead, so he uses this opportunity to glance around for the coyote again.

As he studies the zigzag branches of an oak tree, a faint, almost imperceptible memory taps him in the back of his consciousness. Something happened here once, years ago. Didn't it? Ordinarily, Tomas can look back on any event and perceive almost every detail, instantly. But the memory of this tree appears covered with a thick, white fog. This disturbs him a little, and so he closes his eyes and pushes himself deeper through the meandering haze.

Finally, he comes to the memory, and everything he remembers moves quickly through him, like a movie on fast-forward. He remembers years ago, standing right where is now, seeing the oak tree covered with neon-orange sticky notes. When he stepped forward to get a closer look, he recognized his mother's handwriting on the Post-its. Each one of the notes said, *Walk forward.* And so he did. He walked off the trail, into the thick of the chaparral, where all the ghosts and the red-winged blackbirds lived. The willow tree ahead of him was covered with neon-green sticky notes that told him to keep walking. And so he climbed over glaucous gray boulders. He ducked under burnt-umber branches. And he was never once afraid, because this was where his mother wanted him to go. In the end, he came to a small clearing filled with wildflowers of every color Tomas could imagine. He recognized auburn, tangerine, chartreuse, citron, emerald, ube, lilac, imperial purple.

Standing in the middle of the clearing was Uncle Marvin. He tapped at his chin and said, "Hey, kid. I know you're, you know, perceiving this as a memory, but this is actually a very important message I'm sending you using my special powers. Now, right after I stop talking, I need you to go to your mom and tell her that I gave you a message. Tell her that she needs to kill the helpers right now, or you and your sister will die. And she needs to hurry, all right? She can't even wait a second. She just needs to kill them. I don't mean to scare you, kid, but if you don't tell your mom, then this is going to be you and Ken." And for a moment, Tomas saw his sister and himself standing on either side of Uncle Marv, their skin crumbling off their bones, their eyes rotted away.

The corpses disappeared then, and Uncle Marv said, "Promise me you'll tell her."

"I promise," Tomas said.

The memory dissipates, and Tomas turns to his mother. Usually, when he can feel his tears escaping, he likes to hide and wait. But his dad isn't here to make fun of him, so the boy rushes to his mother. He gives her the messages, and for a moment she only stands there, staring straight ahead, but then she reaches into his jacket pocket. Tomas hears his helper shriek and then go silent.

His mom tosses his helper onto the trail, along with her own, and their mangled, crumpled bodies twitch a little in the lantern light. Tomas's helper stares blankly at the stars with only half a face still attached to his neck.

"Give him to me," Tomas's mom says, turning to Kennedy now.

But Kennedy presses her helper close to her chest and runs toward the dark part of the trail.

"Kennedy!" their mom says.

And Tomas doesn't see what happens next, because darkness fills his vision and he can feel himself falling. In the final seconds before losing consciousness, he worries that maybe he didn't give his mom the message soon enough, and maybe he's going to become that eyeless corpse after all.

## Hendrick

After he falls asleep, Hendrick finds himself crawling on all fours in a dim, cinereous basement. He knows he's looking for a specific object, but he can't quite remember what. The dryer vibrating in the corner wheezes in a way that sounds more human than machine-like. Hendrick creeps away from the dryer, toward the opposite corner of the room, and for the first time, he notices cloudy water spewing through the cracks in the stone walls. The water rushes toward him from every direction. The wheezing of the dryer intensifies. When Hendrick tries to stand, he realizes that the bones of his arms and legs are fused in this position.

The water rises, slowly, and he notices granola-bar wrappers and teeth floating on top. He can hear Imani sloshing through the basement behind him, but when he shifts his body to face her, he sees that this isn't his wife at all. Her long, wavy hair wraps tight around her neck, and he can see a dark emerald eye staring at him between her barely open lips. She grabs her laundry from the dryer and then ascends toward the door. Hendrick knows he should tell her that he's getting too old to stand up, that he needs help with the stairs. But he hesitates for much too long. The water level rises, and by the time he opens his mouth, the murky liquid tumbles down his throat. He can feel the floating teeth lacerating his esophagus and then his stomach from the inside.

When Hendrick opens his eyes, he finds himself sitting on the leather couch, with his feet on the ottoman. "How long was I asleep?" he says.

But Marvin doesn't answer him. Marvin paces the living room, grinding his teeth, tapping hurriedly at each side of his forehead. He moves faster than Hendrick can ever remember seeing him. At one point, he stumbles but manages to catch himself before falling onto his face.

Hendrick must still be half-asleep, because everything in the room appears hazy and chimerical. He shakes his head, trying to revive himself, but nothing changes.

Suddenly, Marvin freezes in place and his head swivels to the side. "Well, they're gone. Forever, I mean. I really don't think they're stupid enough to come back here." His shoulders slump a little, and he rubs at his chin. "I should have observed them more vigilantly, you know? I should have been more careful, but I . . . I let myself get lazy. Relaxed. I guess I'm only good at handling mindless acolytes, but I just . . . I wanted things to be different this time around. I wanted . . . Well, no use crying about it now." He sighs. "I know you don't get what the fuck I'm saying, but it helps to talk sometimes, you know? Even to a boring asshole like you."

Of course, Hendrick doesn't appreciate being called *boring* but he decides to keep his mouth shut. He's better off not picking a fight with the one man in the world who can give him everything. A moment later, Hendrick can't even remember what Marvin said to upset him anymore. The whole situation feels even more dreamlike than before, and Hendrick's having a hard time forming a coherent thought.

Marvin joins him on the couch and absent-mindedly presses buttons on the remote control, even though the TV is off. "I could keep you around, I guess," he says. "But, if I'm being honest with myself, I can't fucking stand you. You think of yourself as some Walter White anti-hero, with your embezzling and your secret apartment, but really, you're just a piece of shit. I mean, the best part of you was Imani and those kids, and you fantasized all the fucking time about what it would be like to throw them away." For a few moments, Marvin wraps his hand tight around the remote control. Then he sighs and lets go. "Well, I guess you have served me okay and all, and you are one of my people. So, I'll try to make this easy on you."

Marvin closes his eyes, and a current of pain cascades down Hendrick's body like a waterfall. His body spasms and then there's only darkness.

When Hendrick opens his eyes again, he finds himself in a room full of salmon-colored fire. The flames cover everything, from the TV screen to the stuffed animal on the floor to the photos on the wall. In the middle of the inferno stands Hendrick's god.

"Well, time to transcend," his god says.

And Hendrick stands, his chest swimming with anticipation. He's been waiting for this day for as long as he can remember. He keeps his arms to his sides, the way he was instructed.

"I'll give you this," the celestial being says. "You do have a pretty decent Blu-ray collection."

"Thank you, my lord."

For a moment, the deity shimmers, and then Hendrick is given one final gift. He gets to see his god's true form. The deity steps forward and coils his sinuous arms around him. The two of them fall sideways now, onto the hardwood floor, but Hendrick hardly registers the pain of the fall. Hendrick stares deep into his god's tiny, sparkling eyes. Over the years, Hendrick would sometimes doubt himself. He would worry that he could never reach the apex of his spiritual development. But now, fully embraced by his god, there's no denying that he has what it takes.

Nearby, one of the small demigods says, "Can we have some?"

"Shush," the deity says. "You're spoiling the mood."

And then the god holds Hendrick even tighter while opening his wide, lipless mouth. The fire fills Hendrick's vision now, and he can feel his own body squirming, but he's not sure why. All his dreams are about to come true.

## *Kennedy*

Kennedy doesn't want to, but she keeps seeing that moment when her mother wrestled away Fantastico and then threw him against the shadowy tree trunk. And she sees Fantastico sprawled on the dirt, his chest cavity popped open like an enormous pimple.

When her mother reaches out to hug her or take her

hand, Kennedy backs away and says, "Stay away from me."

While her mother speaks close to her brother's ear, Kennedy sits by herself on one of the boulders. Ever since the helpers died, Kennedy felt a little lightheaded. Now the giddiness amplifies, and after a few moments, she can't seem to stay upright. So, she shifts herself off the boulder and lies flat on the ground, like Fantastico.

Tears sting her eyes again. She can feel her back pressed flat against the dirt, but at the same time, she feels the sensation of rushing forward, toward the blurry galaxy in front of her. She feels as if the whole planet is increasing speed, pushing her deeper and deeper toward some great unknown or another. The stars swirl in a great swarm of bleeding light. Kennedy knows that she should feel frightened of whatever's happening to her, but the relief she feels overpowers any anxieties that try to form. She feels as if someone's untied her, or pulled the needles from her skin.

The galaxy in front of her waltzes for a few more moments, and then rests at last. The planet pushing at her back finally slows down. Her journey into space feels over, but her inner lightness, the sparkle in her chest, doesn't diminish.

Then Kennedy experiences a little spark of realization, as if waking from a dream that Marv was her uncle. She remembers now that Marvin is only a family friend, an old college buddy of her dad's. And then there's another spark, and she remembers that Marvin was someone her dad worked with. These versions of Marvin continue to burst inside her, until she recalls hiding in the bathroom because a stranger broke into her house. Is that truly who he is? A stranger?

Kennedy worries that maybe she's dying, because in the next few moments, her life flashes before her eyes. She always thought this experience would be like watching a movie on fast-forward, but instead, her mind hops back and forth through time, frenetically and out of her control. She remembers her brother crying uncontrollably on a plane, and her father says, "Shut up. Can you shut him up." Her mother says, "Let me talk to him."

And then Kennedy remembers pressing her foot into wet cement while her father writes her name using a chopstick. She remembers walking around the fake oak tree in Thomas's Bar & Grill. "Somebody took the ugly pineapple man," Tomas yells. "No, he's right there," their mother says, pointing. In another memory, she's lying in bed with the chicken pox, covered with stuffed penguins. This was years ago, back when her father paid more attention to her. In this memory, her father sits beside her and tells her a story about a chicken who also has chicken pox. He even uses silly voices to speak as the chicken and his badger friend. Kennedy remembers Tomas cutting his leg on the haunted trail, and her mom using her own shirt to put pressure on the wound. And she remembers sitting on her bed, playing Drawing Battle. When Tomas leans over to get a good look at her two-headed dragon, he sneezes all over the page.

Sometimes, she remembers a memory and a false memory simultaneously, like when Uncle Marv taught her to ride her bike and when her mom taught her to ride her bike, on the same day, at the same time. And she feels a pressure in her head, like a mild headache, until Marvin's face dissolves away.

Kennedy can't tell how much time passes, but eventually the frenzy of recollections slows down. She feels more in control of her mind again, and when she opens her eyes, the stars appear clear and still and far away. An owl cries out, somewhere in the darkness of the oak woodland beside her.

When she sits up, she notices her mom and her brother lying on the ground, her mom's arm wrapped around him. With her heart beating fast, Kennedy crawls over to them.

"Mom," she says, her voice quivering. She places a hand on her mother's arm. "Mom."

After way too many seconds, her mom's eyes slowly

open. "I'm all right, sweetie," she says. A line of tears sparkle down her mother's face.

"Marvin was tricking us," Kennedy says.

"I know, sweetie."

Kennedy turns her attention to Tomas now, and he stares back at her with wide eyes.

The three of them stand now. Her mom says, "Let's get back to the car. We're going to freeze out here."

"Can't we take their bodies?" Kennedy says. "Maybe they're poisonous or something. Maybe we should bury them somewhere. Please, Mom."

Her mother sighs and says, "Okay."

So, her mother wraps the two small bodies in a handkerchief from her bag, and Kennedy searches for Fantastico near the ancient oak tree. Kennedy remembers now the warning Fantastico gave her in the school bathroom. He wanted her to kill him. He wanted to save her.

She can't see Fantastico's body, but maybe she's remembering the wrong tree? She kneels down and moves a few leaves so that she can see underneath.

Tomas said that Marvin sent him a message and said that they should kill the helpers, but that doesn't make any sense. Why would Marvin set them free after all his work to trick them in the first place? Kennedy remembers then another conversation inside of Uncle Marvin's . . . inside of the guest room. It was right after Fantastico tried to warn her, and Marvin said something like, "When you talked with Ken, you said you should talk to her mom. Did you mess with Imani's brain at all?" And Fantastico said, "I don't know. If I did, I made myself forget about it."

So maybe, that time in the bathroom, when Fantastico was free from Marvin, he did mess with a brain. He messed with Tomas's. He sent a little message into his mind to give them all a chance to escape.

"Leave him, sweetie," her mother says, behind her. "We need to go."

"No!" Tears burn at Kennedy's eyes and she wipes them away frantically so that she can keep looking. Where is his body? Suddenly, another false memory pops in her mind. She remembers now that when her mother wrestled Fantastico away, she didn't throw her helper against the tree. Instead, her mom collapsed on the ground, unconscious. And her brother fell on the ground too.

"Mom!" Kennedy said, rushing forward.

Fantastico stepped out from her mother's hand and straightened his leather jacket. "She'll be fine," he said, looking up at the girl. "I was going to let her squish me, but . . . well. I didn't want you to hate her forever for that. So, I conked her out, but like I said, she'll be fine."

"Why did Marvin say we need to kill you guys?"

Kennedy said, picking him up.

"Well, that was me," he said. "Now that I'm free of Marvin, I can remember tinkering with Tomas a bit." He sighed. "I know none of this makes any sense to you at this point, but I don't have time to explain it right now. When your mom killed those guys, Marvin didn't have time to disconnect from them. Mentally, I mean. So, all that death funneled into Marvin and he passed out. He could wake up at any second, though, so I need to get out of range of you guys as soon as possible. Could you, you know, put me in your brother's car? I need to hurry."

Kennedy didn't understand much of what Fantastico said at that point, but she wanted him to get away. She set him carefully in the small car and placed the remote control on his lap.

"I guess I need to rewrite all this for now," Fantastico said. "So that your mom doesn't come after me. But you'll remember what I'm saying eventually, once I get out of range of you guys. I promise."

He stared up at her for a few more seconds and then pushed the throttle on the remote control. But he stopped almost immediately and turned to face her again. "I just . . . well . . . Thanks for everything, Ken. You're a special kid. And don't worry about me too much, okay? I'll try to get out of Marvin's maximum range before he regains consciousness. Right now, I have a little of my own power inside me, so maybe I'm not just a glorified antenna. I don't know what I'll become out there without him, but I'll try to be something, you know, good." Fantastico waved at her a little then, and she lost consciousness.

Once she recollects all of this, Kennedy turns away from the oak tree and returns to her family.

"I didn't throw yours at the tree," her mother says, fear tugging at her face. "He could still be here."

"He left, Mom," Kennedy says. "He's the one who warned Tomas with that message. I talked to him."

"We'd better go."

The three of them walk back then, the way they came, and her mother holds her hand, squeezing too tight. Kennedy wishes that her mother would make a pun or two, but she never does. She only asks, over and over, if the two of them are all right.

During the walk, Kennedy realizes that now she can explain to Alejandra why she missed her birthday. Marvin probably didn't want anyone to leave the house until he finished creating his antennae. Alejandra probably won't believe a word she says, but she's eager to tell the story anyway.

In the car, her mom makes a call on her cell phone over and over, but no one seems to be answering. Tomas sniffles in his seat.

"We'll be all right now," Kennedy says, and her brother nods. But he still won't stop sniffling.

Eventually, their mom sets down her phone and pulls out of the parking space. As they drive past the shadowy chaparral, Kennedy waves. She knows that Fantastico was made from Marvin. But maybe Fantastico was made from the best part. Maybe her friend will change the trajectory of his existence and do some good out there.

Kennedy can tell, from the direction they're driving, that they're not heading home. She knows her mother must have a plan. And a part of Kennedy wants to ask her mom a hundred questions, but at the same time, she feels exhausted. She closes her eyes, with her brother leaning against her arm, and she dreams that she's one of a dozen witches, flying through a sea of churning stars and planets. She doesn't know exactly where she's headed, but she feels safer knowing that she's not alone facing the horrors of the galaxy. In the end, those horrors don't stand a chance.

# Acknowledgments

My undying gratitude goes to everyone on the Tor.com publishing team who helped spawn this tome, including Lee Harris, Greg Ruth, Greg Manchess, and Christine Foltzer. A big, blinking, neon-green THANK YOU to my loved ones for their continued support. In particular, as writer's block and deadlines and other deadly foes loomed before me, my mom and Lisa swooped in and saved the day with their guidance and encouragement. And, of course, thanks to Bad Movie Club, for their hand in saturating and warping my brain with sublimely god-awful films. Marvin wouldn't have been the same without you.

# About the Author

Photograph by Jacob Shipp

**JEREMY C. SHIPP** is the Bram Stoker Award–nominated author of Cursed, The Atrocities, and Vacation. His shorter tales have appeared in over seventy publications, including Cemetery Dance Magazine, ChiZine, and Pseudopod. Jeremy lives in Southern California in a moderately haunted Victorian farmhouse. His twitter handle is @JeremyCShipp.

# TOR·COM

**Science fiction. Fantasy. The universe.**

**And related subjects.**

\*

More than just a publisher's website, *Tor.com* is a venue for **original fiction, comics,** and **discussion** of the entire field of SF and fantasy, in all media and from all sources. Visit our site today—and join the conversation yourself.